26.X.73

For Jane ⸻

with all
good wishes ⸻

Susan Karin
mengelis

A Thousand Summers

ALSO BY GARSON KANIN

PLAYS

Born Yesterday
The Smile of the World
The Rat Race
The Live Wire
Come On Strong
Musicals
Fledermaus
Do Re Mi
Adaptations
The Amazing Adele
The Good Soup
A Gift of Time

NOVELS

Blow Up a Storm
Do Re Mi
The Rat Race
Where It's At

SHORT FICTION

Cast of Characters (Twenty Stories)

FILMS

The Rat Race
With Ruth Gordon
A Double Life
Adam's Rib
Pat and Mike
The Marrying Kind
In Collaboration
From This Day Forward
The More the Merrier
The True Glory
Original Stories
High Time
The Right Approach
The Girl Can't Help It
Original Screenplays
It Should Happen to You
Where It's At
Some Kind of Nut

NONFICTION

Tracy and Hepburn
Remembering Mr. Maugham
Felix Frankfurter: A Tribute (*Contributor*)

A Thousand Summers

By Garson Kanin

Doubleday & Company, Inc.
Garden City, New York
1973

ISBN: 0-385-06973-1
Library of Congress Catalog Card Number 73-79679
Copyright © 1973 by T.F.T. Corporation
All Rights Reserved
Printed in the United States of America
First Edition

Upon those who love,
Ungenerous time bestows
A thousand summers.

A Thousand Summers

I

IN THOSE DAYS, if you got something in your eye,
you headed for the nearest drugstore. There, the druggist would remove it. In some instances, he would then
wash the eye, or bandage it if it was scratched, or apply
an ointment, or sell you something, or nothing, or charge
a fee (usually a quarter) or not.

Freeman smelled her before he ever saw her. The
scent was uncommon, and so powerful that it cut
through the antiseptic odor of his drugstore, a small,
resort-town establishment in Edgartown, on the island
of Martha's Vineyard, Massachusetts.

He was in the back room when he heard the musical
bell that signaled the entrance of a customer. A moment
later, he became aware of that scent. Normally, he
would have called out and asked the customer to wait
until he had finished compounding the prescription on
his table. ("And *never*—do you hear me, son?—*never*,
no matter what-all, let *anything* interfere with the completion of the filling of the prescription. You'll come
back to it and pick it up fine ninety-nine times and
then the hundredth, you'll err and somebody'll die before their time because of you. Learn the rules and

stick to 'em!'") He had adhered to this as he had to all of his father's superior advice, but this time he committed the single exception. That scent! He knew it belonged to a stranger, which made him curious. Further, it seemed a night aroma and incongruous at this early hour. He had opened the store no more than fifteen minutes earlier.

He put aside his mortar and pestle, rinsed his hands, dried them—why was his heart pounding?—and walked out into the shop.

A one-eyed woman stood at the counter. His being responded with the awe invariably inspired by pure beauty. A tremor, gooseflesh.

"Good morning," he said, his voice sounding odd to him.

"I'm afraid I've got something in my eye." Her hand —long, delicate, lovely—came down from her face. She had two eyes, after all. "Can you get it out?"

He studied her, looking for a flaw, until she repeated, "*Can* you?"

"I can try," he said, and added, "Good morning."

"Good morning," she echoed and laughed a perfect laugh. "You *are* Mr. Osborn, then? The pharmacist?"

He thought it best not to speak again since his voice had gone so loony. Instead, nodding, he beckoned her into the back room and then beyond that into his small office.

As he moved, he checked himself in the mirror. Thank God, this was one of his handsome days. He was often told how attractive he was, but could not see it— except on certain days when he held his tall figure erect, groomed himself carefully, and lifted himself out of habitual melancholy. On these occasions, he noted, his eyes turned from gray to blue.

He closed the door and pointed to a straight chair beside the shelves that held a collection of Japanese Kokeshi dolls. He wondered if she would ask about them. Visitors to this room were rare, but the dolls were often conversation pieces. He twisted a goose-necked lamp into position, switched on the light to test its throw, switched it off, and went to his cabinet. There he prepared an absorbent cotton-tipped tooth-pick, got out a fresh hand towel, and brought them to the desk beside her. He moved to the washbasin and began to scrub his hands in the manner of a surgeon. He blushed as he realized he was showing off.

"This is most kind of you," she said.

"Not at all." (Voice still wavy, damn it!)

"It happened over an hour ago. I've just been waiting for you to open."

"You should've knocked."

"Oh?"

"Here. On the rear door. I'm always here by seven."

"Seven!"

"Yes. Gives me a couple of hours for this and that before I open the store."

"Well," she said. "Next time."

"Oh, no. Let's hope there won't be a next time."

"No."

"Nasty things, cinders."

He came to her. She lifted her face to him. He stood close to her. His thigh touched her body. He began to

3

tremble and wondered if he was going to be able to perform the simple operation.

He took her head gently into his hands, and moved it into position. He picked up the swab.

"Now, let's see," he said. "Can you feel it?"

"Yes. When I blink."

"Left, right? High or low?"

She blinked, winced, and said, "I can't tell. Sorry."

"No matter."

He slipped a headband, which held a magnifier, over his head. He placed two fingers, carefully, above and below her eye. He moved his head closer to hers.

"Ah!" he exclaimed. "There it is."

"Thank you."

"Not yet. Now. Please hold still. Still as you can."

"Yes."

"Wet this, please."

He held the swab close to her lips. She took it into her mouth, released it.

Freeman moved the swab close to her eye, felt her grow tense, but continued and brushed the swab lightly over the cornea of her eye.

A cry escaped her and she pulled away.

"Did I hurt you?" he asked.

"Yes, you did." She blinked and said with no little exasperation, "And it's still *there!*"

They exchanged a look to which she contributed irritation, and he, dismay.

She began to rise. He put his hand on her shoulder.

"Not again," she said. "Please. It really is *too* painful."

4

"I know. That's a badly insulted eye."

"What am I to do?" she asked despairingly.

"Nothing," he said firmly. "I'll do it."

He dropped the swab, snatched off the magnifier, threw it aside, stepped close to her, took her head in his hands.

"What are you doing?" she asked. "—Going to do?"

He did not reply. Instead, acting with resolution and force, he lowered his head to hers. One hand moved to hold open her eye, the other steadied her head. Now he brought his mouth above her eye and, all at once, brushed his tongue over it. She gasped. His tongue moved again; licking (caressing?), cleansing her eye. Again. Again.

He released her and stepped away, flushed and excited.

She, conversely, had turned pale and appeared to be speechless.

When finally she found her voice, she said, "It's out! I think." She blinked several times, stood up and said, "Yes! It is. Oh, I *do* thank you." She went to him impulsively and put her hand on his arm. "I'm grateful to you—beyond the power of expression. *Lord*, what a relief!"

"Thank Sergeant Hufstader," he said.

"Who?"

"The old army regular who taught it to me. That technique. He told me *he'd* learned it in Mexico—from an Aztec water boy—during the Spanish-American War. A dusty one, apparently."

He led her to the basin and prepared an eyecup.

5

"What's that?" she asked.

"Boric acid solution. You'd better bathe it three or four times a day for a day or two."

She smiled. "You'll have to be more specific, I'm afraid. I'm the literal type."

"Morning, afternoon, and evening," he said. "For the next four days."

"Like this?"

She put her eye into the eyecup and let her head fall back.

He became aware of her finely sculptured profile, the flowing lines of her long neck, and her closer-to-red-than-brown auburn hair. He looked at the outline of her breasts and found it difficult to take his eyes from their promise. And that skin. The scent.

"That's fine," he said.

He handed her a towel. She dried her face and handed it back.

"What do I owe you?" she asked.

He looked at her for a long time before he answered, "A quarter."

They moved slowly, together, from the office into the back room and from there into the still-deserted drugstore.

He took his place behind the cash register. She gave him a dollar. He gave her the change.

"Thank you again," she said. "I think I'd rather have a *baby* than something in my eye."

"Have you ever?"

"Had a baby?"

"Yes."

"No," she said.

"I thought not. Or you wouldn't say that."

"I suppose *you have* had a baby."

"My wife. And it's more trouble than a cinder, I assure you. And takes longer."

"And costs more than a quarter," she said.

"Yes."

They laughed together.

"By the way," she said, "what happened to the cinder?"

"Inside me," he said. "Thank you."

She made ready to leave. He could not bear the idea.

"May I offer you some refreshment?" he asked. "Our soda fountain here is rarin' to go."

"No, thank you."

"You've just been through an ordeal. Maybe you should."

"I *could* do with a sip of water," she said.

He went behind the fountain, she moved to it. He suppressed a cry of exultation as she hoisted herself gracefully up onto one of the tall, bent-iron fountain chairs.

"You sure you wouldn't rather ginger ale?" he asked.

"Quite sure."

"Checkerberry soda?"

"No, thank you."

"Homemade root beer?"

"Whose home?"

"Mine."

"Is that true?"

"Swear to God," he said. "I make the root beer myself."

7

"In that case," she said, "I *will* have some."

He prepared to serve it as he said, "I thought if I was going to have a fountain, I ought to have at least *one spécialité de la maison.*" He put the glass before her. "*Voilà! Madame est servie!*"

"You speak French," she noted.

"Yes. My wife is French," he explained. "I might say *extremely* French."

"How nice."

"Is it?"

"Isn't it?"

"My wife is very nice when she's in France, but here—"

"Mr. Osborn!"

"Yes?"

"I think you're forgetting I'm a perfect stranger."

"Perfect, yes," he heard himself say. "Stranger, no."

She finished her root beer swiftly, slipped from the chair, and reached into her purse. He shook his head and waved his palm from side to side. She started out.

At the door, she turned back to him, smiled, and said, "Morning, afternoon, and evening. For four days."

Those were her words, but they seemed to convey another meaning. He was not sure what it was.

He watched her go through the door and up the street, keeping his eyes on her until he could no longer see her.

He washed the glass she had used, fingering it sensuously. The scent of her was still about. He replaced the glass on its shelf.

He started for the back room to resume his work, but stopped and clutched the counter as he felt himself go weak. Two thoughts had struck him with force at the same moment: He loved her. He did not know her name.

Suppose she never . . .

II

. . . REMEMBERING ALL THIS, the old man began to cry.

His porch-mate, who had been rocking in the chair beside him, rose discreetly and shuffled away to the other side of the long porch. This is the established protocol at the Falmouth Sunset House on Cape Cod, Massachusetts. The privacy of misery is respected, and it has long been understood, by guests and attendants alike, that there is nothing, in any case, to be done. They know that old people weep at many things: a sudden pang of memory, a severe pain, a wisp of an itch, a sense of being bereft, anger at the body's unwillingness to respond to an order, frustration, loneliness, disappointment in the undone or loose ends or lost opportunities, the irritation of muddled memory; above all, at the inevitability of what lies so close ahead, or at the immutable permanence of what has gone before.

Here it has been learned that they cannot be comforted. They cry themselves out, as they did when they were infants and cried for more innocent reasons.

Moreover, in the elderly, the tear-producing mechanism has lost resilience, the ducts have shrunk or begun

9

to atrophy, crying is mechanically less practical than it has been, and the needed energy is in short supply. Thus, as a rule, the spell soon ends.

The old man blew his nose, glanced over at his recent companion, and nodded reassuringly. He put away his handkerchief and looked out at the sea. It was blue-gray today. The last of his tears blurred the friendly sight and assisted the recovery of memory in the way that dimness or darkness bridges the journey to sleep.

Fighting disorientation, he placed himself in time. He was seventy-nine, or as he sometimes preferred to put it—"in my eightieth year." He saw his signature before him: "Freeman T. Osborn." Unlike most signatures, it was clean and clear and perfectly legible; a copybook example of Palmer Method penmanship. His father, anachronistically permissive about most aspects of child rearing, had bullied him about this single detail.

"If you're going to be a pharmacist—and you are— then, by God, you'd better look to it and set down a hand that can be read by all. The damned M.D.s can scribble—and most of them do—but don't *you*. You're setting down vital records—and 'vital' means life or death. What's more, people who write clear, think clear. Those sloppy scrawlers are, by God, drawing you a picture of the macaw's nest inside their heads!"

Freeman smiled as he played back the sound of the familiar voice, vibrant and fresh, although his father had been dead for almost fifty years.

Pharmacy. Had he ever considered anything else? Probably not, other than the standard ballplayer-fire-man-beekeeper-fisherman-explorer visions. It was almost as though he had been *born* a pharmacist, in the way that a prince is born a prince.

He reviewed a succession of signs over the entry of the corner store that had been the major post of his life:

THE EDGARTOWN PHARMACY
Seth M. Osborn, Prop.

THE EDGARTOWN PHARMACY
Seth M. Osborn, Prop.
Freeman T. Osborn, Pharm.

THE EDGARTOWN PHARMACY
Seth Osborn and Son, Props.

EGARTOWN DRUG STORE
F. T. Osborn, Pharmacist

OSBORN'S
Drugs—Sundries—Sodas

EDGARTOWN DISCO DRUG
(Formerly Osborn's)

He discarded the last two and moved back in time to the Edgartown Drug Store days on the island that he could see from here, on clear days. This was the part of his memory world in which he felt, at the same time, more at ease and more alive.

He picked up the thread of his remembrance, reflecting that it was now the core of his existence. Well, hell. At least he had something to remember. Not everyone did. Sheila. He smiled, recalling that on that first day he had failed to learn her name. Sheila. What a meeting! And what a waiting for the second. He remembered that four endless days had passed before she . . .

III

. . . FREEMAN HAD REVIEWED the extraordinary adventure many times during the next four days and nights. His wife was away on one of her periodic trips to France, and he was living the solitary life to which he had become, in succession: accustomed, resigned, attached. Until now. Now he was stirred with longing for more than his days and nights held. Who was this intoxicating woman? His position in the small town was such that he could make only the most discreet inquiries. They garnered nothing.

On the fifth day, at 7:15 A.M., there was a sharp knock on his back door. He opened it. She stood there, surpassing even his idealized memory. She wore white, and a single yellow rose in her bodice.

"May I come in?" she asked.

"Of course."

She went at once to the straight chair and sat.

"Which eye is it this time?" he asked.

"Neither. Both."

He locked the door and went to her. They kissed. It seemed to them a perfectly natural expression. It was as though they had kissed many times before.

"Thank you," she said. "Although that is not what I came for."

"No?"

"Not entirely," she said. "I wanted to ask you about that remarkable collection of Kokeshi dolls."

He sat down near her.

"You know about Kokeshi dolls?" he asked.

"Why, yes. Why does that surprise you?"

"Because in the five years I've been collecting them, you're the first person ever to know—well, even what they *are*."

"We did a tour of duty in Japan—three years. I have some Kokeshis of my own. Not as fine as yours, I'm afraid."

"Choose one. Please. I want you to have it."

She looked over at the dolls, and said, "I'm meant to say 'no,' of course, but I believe I'll say 'yes.' Or, as I've heard in this part of the country—'Don't mind if I do!'"

She went to the collection, studied it carefully, and finally selected a small, exquisitely wrought, and subtly painted doll.

"This one," she said.

"Bravo."

"Why?"

"It's the best one," he said. "The most valuable."

"I know."

She came to him, said, "Thank you," bent down and kissed him. She resumed her chair and asked, "Have you been to Japan?"

"Not yet," he said. "It's one of my dreams."

"Be prepared for another world," she said. "The Japanese—not only do they *think* in different categories, but they *feel* in them."

"Go on, please."

"Well, you know all this, probably—but they relate

13

to death, for instance, not as we do—in prevailing thought. To them, death is not the *end* of life, but a *part* of life."

"Never mind life and death," he said. "Tell me about those mixed communal baths."

"The water is very hot."

"Did you do it?" he asked. "Go?"

"Of course."

"Good God."

"Not without a certain amount of unease, I confess. But you know the saying, 'When in Kyoto—.' "

In the next half hour, between increasingly passionate kisses, he learned that her name had been Sheila Hanrahan, that she was now Mrs. Thomas Van Anda, wife of a man high up in the Foreign Service, that they were here for the summer, that she was in need of companionship.

Later, Freeman prepared coffee and they sat—he, back to his roll-top desk; she, in a nearby armchair.

"May I compliment you on your coffee?" she asked. "It's outstanding."

"Thank you. All compliments gratefully received. You must remember, though, that I'm a chemist of sorts. I prepare coffee the same as I do a prescription. Also, I'm a superb cook."

"*Are* you?"

"Yes, my wife's away a good deal of the time, and I find it best to do for myself. I don't much like ordering in advance."

"Nor I, if it can be helped."

"Then, too," he continued, "I'm partial to Japanese food—and Island ladies grow pale at the sight of anyone

14

eating *sashimi.* I've pointed out that it's only *raw* fish—while they cheerfully slurp oysters and clams—*live* fish. But it makes no impression."

"We get so set in our ways, don't we?"

"What's worse is that we get set in our *parents'* ways. It's taken me years to shake off some of my father's. More coffee?"

"Please."

He laughed lightly as he poured a second cup for her and said, "I'm the sole owner of this emporium here. My father insisted I buy him out. You'll never guess why."

"Tell me."

He handed her the cup and kissed her.

"Thank you," she said. "And thank you."

"The soda fountain. It seemed inevitable, but he put it off from year to year. Finally, as his partner, I had to tell him the time had come. We couldn't buck the trend any longer. And he said, 'Well, then. It's me or the gadget, son. You can't have both. I'm a pharmacist, damn it all, not a confectioner—and I won't be both! It's up to you.' Well, painful as it was, I had to choose the gadget, as he called it. And bought him out. He drove a hard bargain, and I suspect I paid too much. Still, I respected his Yankee trading. And him. He died only two years ago. Before that, he'd come in almost every day for, guess what? Right. For an ice-cream soda. He ordered his pharmaceuticals from Otis Clapp & Son in Boston—because they had no soda fountains in any of their . . . Is *your* father alive?"

"Yes. Wyoming. Cattle."

"Brothers? Sisters?"

"Two brothers, both older—with my father. One sister, younger. She lives in Rome and we're out of touch. We quarreled over a legacy—my mother's—and never made it up. I'm sure we never will. I was right, incidentally, and she was wrong."

"Of course."

"I'm afraid I don't cook at all," she said, frowning. "I've never had to learn. Do you think less of me?"

"Yes, but no matter. I'll do the cooking."

There was a long pause before she whispered, "You will?"

"I'll do everything," he said. "Anything. When the time comes. When our time comes."

They shared a long silence.

"I'm a superlative photographer," she said.

"Good. You can take pictures of me cooking."

They laughed.

"Wait!" she said.

"What?"

"I just remembered. There *is* something I can do in the way of food. It's not cooking, precisely, but it *is* something."

"Such as?"

"It's called an *ensoku*," she said.

"Of course," he said. "A picnic."

"How do you know that?"

"My dearest love," he said, "you'll learn, in time, that I know much more about Japan and the Japanese than you do. Even though I've never been there. Maybe *because* I've never been there. I've read the books and memorized the maps and studied the history and ab-

16

sorbed the art—and, of course, my Kokeshis. I've learned a lot from them."

"When shall we have our *ensoku?*"

"Our *first ensoku*," he said, correcting her.

"Yes. Our *first ensoku*."

"Whenever you say."

She frowned in thought. "Let me see. On the first— that's in two weeks—my husband goes to Washington for a five-day conference. One of those days?"

"All of them," he said.

"We can't picnic every day," she said.

"Why not? The way I see it, our whole *life* together is going to be a picnic. Speaking of your husband—"

"Yes?"

"Where does he think you are now? At this moment?"

"My husband sleeps till noon. Except on those rare occasions when something unavoidable or unpostponable occurs in the morning hours. He reads—he writes —late into the night. It's his way. He's a night person. A 'nyctophile' he calls himself. He's become a New Yorker. That explains it. A night place. They spend the days there getting ready for the nights. But I grew up on a ranch—was born there, in fact. *Our* days began with the light and ended with the dark."

"There's a lot to be said for the dark," he said.

"Oh, I'm sure of it. I thought we were talking about influences—why we are as we are."

"I don't care *why* you are. I'm just grateful to God that you *are*."

"I'll have to phone New York for some of the things. The fish here, I suppose."

"Yes."

"Poole's?"

"I'll get it," he said.

"No, no. Please. I *want* to. I can't tell you how important it is to me."

He stood up quickly and said, "Squibnocket Pond."

"I beg your pardon?"

"It all comes clear," he said. "Don't tell me there's no design in the way things happen. Or no guiding intelligence. There is—*must* be."

"Of course."

"Listen to this," he said, moving closer to her. "Six years ago—no, seven—a few months after I came home from France and the Army—I bought these nineteen acres on Squibnocket Pond—that's way up-Island, near Gay Head. No sense to it. I read an ad in the *Gazette*, drove over, and said yes on the spot. An impulse—and so unexplainable that I didn't even try to explain it to my wife—my *new* wife, she was, at that time."

"Nineteen acres."

"Most of it wooded—but the pond is grand—and there's access to the sea. But what I loved about it—on sight—was that it put me in mind of Japan—of photographs I'd seen, and prints: Hokusai, Hiroshige, Harunobu. The light, I imagine, and for some reason, the foliage. Hundreds of little bonsai trees underfoot—or what might be bonsai. Some of the plants *may* be Japanese, for all I know."

"But how *could* they be?"

"Don't you know about our island? We're the *world*. We're pretty cosmopolitan—though we seem to be country bumpkins leading bucolic lives."

"Not at all."

"But our fathers and grandfathers and the ones before used it as a base, mostly. For the most part, they were off in the world, out at sea—whaling and trading and, of course, bringing back souvenirs and mementos."

"Yes, I know. I've come upon some beautiful things."

"Have you seen our pagoda tree? The one on South Water?"

"I've seen many trees, but—"

"Come on," he said. "I'll show you."

They left the office and walked a block and a half up the still deserted street. As they approached the tree, he took her arm and stopped her.

"There it is."

"Yes," she said. "I've seen it—and admired it—but—"

"A pagoda tree."

He led her closer to it until she could read the descriptive wooden plaque:

GIANT PAGODA TREE
(A Chinese Huai Tree Sophora Japonica)
Brought from China in a flower
pot in 1837, by Captain Thomas Milton
to grace his new home then being built.
This is believed to be the largest of
its kind on this continent.

"Think of it!" she exclaimed and grasped his arm as though to root herself, for the moment, in the present.

As they walked back to the store, he went on. "And Beetlebung Corner. Have you been there—seen it?"

"I'm afraid not."

"I'll take you," he said. "It's something to see."

"Where is it?"

"Out toward—well, hell!—we'll stop there when we go to Squibnocket. It's right on the way."

"Lovely."

"A whole clump of beetlebung trees—brought to the Island, I suppose, the way the pagoda was."

"And that's why you think the ones on your land may be—?"

"Oh, I don't know," he said. "It may be imagination. Still. It means something to me."

"Are you all right?" she asked.

"Why?"

"You've gone pale," she said.

"Yes. I *feel* pale."

They returned to his office. He went out to the back room and returned with a small bottle of aromatic spirits. He removed the top and sniffed it.

"What my mother used to call 'the vapors.' I'd feel ridiculous if I fainted at your feet."

"Please don't," she said.

"It's just that I'm—what shall I say?—*overwhelmed* by the supernaturalness of it all. Working in chemistry, a man tends to become materialistic—but this—there's no explanation for it. No. That's not what I mean. There *is* an explanation for it and that's what makes it— what did I say?—yes—overwhelming."

He sniffed the bottle again.

"I'm not sure I follow," she said, frowning.

He reached over and gently removed the frown from her forehead with his thumb.

"Look. Seven years ago, on an impulse, I bought a piece of land. I didn't need it—or want it, particularly.

I had no use for it. I haven't been there more than half a dozen times in all these years. A Japanese spot, I thought it was. And then—a certain cinder—infinitesimal—blows into a particular eye—and the design is complete. I bought the land for us, my darling—I've been holding it—waiting for us. Some part of me knew —without knowing—that you were on the way. Sheila."

She reached out and touched him. He took her hand and kissed it and said . . .

IV

. . . ON THE PORCH IN FALMOUTH, the season had changed. Late autumn contained intimations of a harsh winter to come.

The old Freeman sat, wearing an overcoat, hat, and gloves.

The attendants had long ago given up trying to control him. He was one of those stubborn, independent, ownway creatures.

He was alone on the porch, which suited him perfectly. The consecutiveness of mind he had cultivated with effort thrived on solitude, suffered when interrupted or distracted.

Lucky, he thought. Lucky she came in when she did. A few years earlier (years and days were interchangeable now), and it might have been his father who would have dealt with the cinder in her eye. Thank you, God.

Yes.

His father had retired in 1920, at the age of sixty. Freeman recalled that sixty, at that time, was considered an advanced age. Freeman had returned from the war, which he had greatly enjoyed, having been stationed in Paris for virtually his full term of service as Master Sergeant-Pharmacist at the A. E. F. Base Headquarters Hospital. There, he had met and married Colette, the daughter of a distinguished French obstetrician, Dr. Paul-Louis de Vallande.

He had brought her home to Edgartown, which she loathed on sight. It was a normal reaction to displacement, he had thought, and was certain that the condition would change in time. He was wrong. Colette never made the adjustment, fell ill constantly, became a perennial invalid, fully occupied with her maladies and their treatment, and seemed to live only for her frequent returns to France. A month each year, at first. Later, a season each year. When, in 1939, World War II interfered, she took to traveling elsewhere. Canada, Mexico, South America. When the war ended, she went to France and stayed for a year to make up for lost time. For the rest of her married life, she spent half of each year at home and the other half abroad. This seemed to her a fair, even a generous, arrangement. She died in 1959 at the age of sixty-three, when the small plane carrying her from Paris to the Côte d'Azur crashed a few miles south of Avignon, in a sudden, violent thunderstorm.

She had successfully staved off motherhood for four

years after her marriage, but in 1925, a faulty pessary betrayed her and she found, to her horror, that she was pregnant. She did not inform Freeman, but made plans at once to leave for France and consult with her father about means of aborting the unwanted birth. She knew, of course, that there was no one in the United States competent to deal with the matter.

Dr. de Vallande's reaction astonished her—she knew him no better than she knew her husband—and she found herself forced to bear her child under his constant and overbearing supervision.

Freeman went to Paris to be present at the birth of their daughter, Jacqueline. He had fought hard to have the child born in America, but lost.

Poor Jacqueline. She was to endure a childhood compounded of disapproval, neglect, and systematic rejection from a mother who resented her existence.

Her father, attempting to compensate, smothered her with too many things, an overabundance of attention, and succeeded in spoiling her. By the time she was sixteen and in high school, she was a nervous admixture of self-doubt and arrogance, shyness and aggressiveness, joy and misery.

Odd, thought Freeman, that it had all turned out so well. There she was now, in Denver, working with her eminent husband and so concentratedly involved that she emerged from their laboratory only for summers in Chilmark, on the Vineyard; or for special occasions, one of which she believed to be the Christmas trip to see her father.

Freeman remembered her visit this past Christmas. She had been deeply troubled by his move to the Falmouth Sunset House. He tried to explain the reasons, without success. It seemed to her to be a living death. He agreed, secretly, but insisted that it was the most practical arrangement. She informed him that she would not come again. The experience would be too painful. No, next year he would come to see her and Max and the boys in Denver. They would have a proper Christmas, not one of these damned plastic nonsenses.

He smiled as he reflected that he could hardly wait until next Christmas to see if it would come about. He would make a bet with himself. How much? He began to laugh.

He stopped as he realized that he was being observed from either side. A man who cries and laughs in the course of five minutes must surely be regarded as peculiar.

What had he been crying about? It took him a straining time to bring it back to mind. His year in prison? No, that was part of *yesterday's* remembering. The photograph this morning in the *Vineyard Gazette*. The Japanese house. Squibnocket Pond. The visit. Those people. Had it happened or was memory determined to torture him? Sheila. That second meeting, so full of promise. He had known that they would meet again on the following day. There are no half-miracles. He remembered how wrong he had been, how terrified when he . . .

V

. . . Sheila did not appear on the following day, although he had been certain that she would. To that end, he had brought from his house a treasured Crown Derby coffee service and a hand-wrought silver tray.

He had had his hair cut and had carefully trimmed his fingernails.

A few of his regular customers noted, throughout the day, that Freeman was uncharacteristically testy. He failed to respond to the habitual banter and grew increasingly morose.

Ollie Luce, the waggish harbormaster, came in at five.

"Lemme have three youknowwhats, Doc. They're not for me, y'unnerstan'. For my kids. And Tilton's fresh outa balloons."

He laughed uproariously. He was always his own best audience. He stopped when he realized that Freeman had not joined him.

"Here you are," said Freeman, serving him.

"What's a matter, boy? You sick?"

"Yes," Freeman replied.

"Something serious?"

"Yes."

"What?"

"Nothing."

"But serious?"

"Yes."

"Jesus!"

"See you, Ollie."

Freeman returned to the back room.

Ollie swiped a box of Sen-Sen from the counter and left.

The next day, Sheila came in through the front entrance in the midafternoon, accompanied by a tall, portly, clearly important man who wore an old blazer with a Yale pocket-patch.

"Mr. Osborn," Sheila said, "this is my husband, Thomas Van Anda."

"How do you do?"

"How do you do?"

Freeman was relieved that they were not standing close enough to make a handshake mandatory.

"Mr. Osborn, Thomas, is the gentleman who helped me with my eye."

"Yes," said her husband absently. He was looking about the shop, obviously for nothing in particular.

That "Thomas" struck Freeman's ear. Why not "Tom"? Why not "dear"?

Sheila took a shopping list from her bag and handed it to Freeman.

"Do you mind?" she asked. "It seems so much easier."

Purple ink on pale yellow paper. The handwriting: small, perfectly placed on the page, delicate. When, he wondered, would he find the first flaw in this creature?

He began to fill the order, at the same time observing her husband. Two pints of Dickinson's Witch Hazel. Van Anda's hair was white; not gray, white. A bottle of one hundred aspirin tablets. His slightly puffed face was the kind Freeman associated with drinking men. Five Gillette safety-razor blades. He appeared to be distant, preoccupied, bemused. One quart of rubbing alcohol. From time to time, he inhaled and exhaled in a way that betrayed weariness and the heavy weight of responsibility. A tin of Lyon's tooth powder. Freeman was good at guessing ages, and placed Van Anda in the forty-to-forty-five range. A box of Smith Brothers Cough Drops. He knew, as well as he knew anything, that Sheila was thirty. Tincture of iodine. He decided to guess his own age. Thirty-four? Right! One large jar of Vaseline. That scent of hers was making him giddy again.

"Will that be all?" he asked.

"Thomas? Anything?"

"Nothing. Come along."

Van Anda floated out of the store, the bell reverberated. Freeman wondered why it had had another sound on the day it had preceded her first appearance.

"This is going to be heavy," he said. "Let me send it to you."

"No, no," she said. "We can manage. My husband will carry it."

"Will he?"

"Of course."

"Tomorrow?" he asked softly.

"Tomorrow," she replied.

VI

At 7:00 a.m., when they met, they could not speak of themselves, nor of their plans. The news of Charles A. Lindbergh's successful solo flight to Paris had come through. Ronnie Pease, a schoolboy who lived two doors from Freeman, had built a crystal radio set the year before and this morning had heard the news announced over WGY, Schenectady, as well as KDKA, Pittsburgh. He ran to Freeman's and told him at breakfast. When Freeman repeated it to Sheila, she wondered if she should awaken her husband to tell *him*.

"Better not," advised Freeman. "It may not be true. If it is, it'll be in the papers when they arrive this afternoon. Of course, we *could* telephone the *Boston Globe*."

They did so and confirmed the information. All other events and subjects seemed, for the time, dwarfed by the momentous achievement.

What would it mean in terms of the future? How long before it would be routine? Would passengers be carried across the seas by airplanes in their lifetime? Would *you* go? Would *you?*

It was an exciting day.

The next day, the Lindbergh story having become a reality, they returned to themselves and to one another.

Freeman, with persistent questioning, elicited the story of her life up to now.

28

The ranch and the thirty-mile-away school. The agony and loneliness of boarding school in Denver, Colorado. The year of chaperoned travel, with her Aunt Rhoda. The shipboard romance with the First Officer. The decision to go to college. Wellesley and why. The sudden awakening of social consciousness as a result of a campus lecture by Jane Addams of Hull House, Chicago. Her summer at Hull House. Her wartime job with the Manpower Commission in Washington. The important government official who attempted to seduce her and failed. The less important government officer who attempted to seduce her and succeeded. Her meeting with Thomas Van Anda. His proposal. Her trip back to Wyoming to think it over. Her return. Her acceptance. Japan, France, Denmark, Venezuela, Washington. Here.

Freeman thanked her for sharing the details of her life. He needed them desperately in order to establish his own place in it.

On the following day, the tables were turned, and Freeman told her everything about himself that she wanted to know.

What interested her more than anything else was the subject of his aspiration. What was his aim? A second pharmacy? A chain of them, perhaps?

"God, no," he said. "I've no ambitions in the business line. I'm afraid I'm not much of a businessman—not interested in it. Does that trouble you?"

"What *are* you good at?"

"Bluefishing, chemistry, and loving you."

"Chemistry. What do you do about it?"

"What I'd like to do," he said, "is put together just

29

one damned thing that'd be useful. I don't aim as high as a cure for the common cold—but—"

"Why not?"

"Well," he shrugged. "*You* know. But one thing. Suppose I could find something that would keep insects out of a house or off of people. An antidote for ptomaine. A harmless pain reliever. That's it! That's what I want to do—relieve pain or discomfort in some way."

"Yes," she said, studying him and finding a new dimension of his personality.

"There's so damn much pain in the world. Too much. We get smart at so many things. Sometimes—most often —the wrong things. We fly across the ocean, but we can't stop the croup."

"Of course we can," she said. "Just give us time."

"Time," he echoed.

VII

VAN ANDA LEFT FOR WASHINGTON. Car to Vineyard Haven, ferry to Woods Hole, train to New York, change trains, to Washington.

Sheila accompanied him to the ferry. When it had sailed, she dismissed the car and began a day of shopping.

Freeman told Mrs. Petschek, his part-time helper, that he was going to the jobber's headquarters on the Cape for supplies, and gave her lock-up instructions.

Mrs. Petschek was a registered pharmacist who had

been with Caswell-Massey in New York City for twenty-two years. She had come to the Island seven years earlier to spend her two-week vacation and decided to stay on. She made arrangements to keep her room at Captain Cauldwell's Guest House on an annual basis and did not return to New York. In fact, since her arrival, she had not left the Island.

"Why should I?" she said. "Where's it better than here?"

Her deal with Freeman was casual and informal and suited them both. She came in to assist or to take over whenever Freeman needed her.

He put the elaborate wicker picnic basket that Sheila had delivered at seven that morning into the back of his Nash, and drove to Vineyard Haven via the shore route. He wanted the air.

At the appointed hour (11:15 A.M.), he drove by a prearranged spot (the small bridge on Howard Avenue). Sheila was strolling across it slowly. He drove up beside her and stopped.

"Good morning."

"Good morning."

"Can I give you a lift?" he asked.

"Undoubtedly," she replied and got in beside him.

He took a circuitous route. Not for secrecy, there was no need for that, but because he wanted to show his love some parts of the Island she might not have seen. Up the North Road to Tea Lane and left, down toward the sea. Through the hills of Chilmark on toward Gay Head and, suddenly, another left turn into a wood. Turns and twists and careful maneuvering and, finally, a locked gate. Freeman left the car, unlocked the gate, drove the car through, relocked the gate, and continued.

"We're home," he said.

"It's beautiful," she said. "But it's not Japan."

"Wait."

An old, stone wall and beyond it, a rock garden. Then a wild copse, and a few yards on, a small glade.

They left the car. She walked away from him to explore. He watched her as she looked about, bent down, disappeared from sight, reappeared, touched a tree, and returned to him.

"Yes," she said. "It is. Thank you."

They walked together.

"They're not bonsais," she said. "But close enough."

"Confession," he said. "I'm responsible for the surrounding cherry trees."

"I know of nothing more enchanting," she said.

"And as Al Jolson says, 'You ain't seen *nuthin'* yet!'"

He took her hand and led her on a tour of his domain. It took the better part of an hour. They traveled the path to the pond, and he showed her the easy access to the open sea. On the way back, he promised her a surprise. "You've seen our sea. I've shown you our pond."

"Yes."

"Now here—is our pool."

Suddenly, in a thicket, there it was. So splendidly arranged, it might have been man-made, except that man would have been more modest and made it not quite so large. It was enclosed by bushes and shrubs, and had a mossy bank. The water, gushing up from springs, was crystal clear.

"We can swim in it," he said, "if you like. After lunch."

"Really?" she said, and kicked off her shoes. "But that's so long to wait. And most unhealthy, they say." She bent down and brought her dress up over her head. Standing in her slip, she continued. "Aren't you supposed to wait at least an hour? After lunch, I mean." The slip came off, and the chemise. The brassiere and the garter belt and the stockings.

Freeman stood, agape, seeing double. He closed his eyes hard, opened them. Still double. Of course. She in her surpassing nakedness, and her reflection in the pool.

And now she was in the pool, swimming about as though it had been built around her. Floating on her back, undulating gently through the still waters, blending with enveloping nature.

Freeman found himself in the water beside her, although he could not remember undressing.

They swam together, touched, embraced, kissed. They exchanged the warmth and the pressure of their bodies in the cold water. They reveled in the sense of feeling welcomed by nature—welcomed back.

They came out of the pool, hand in hand, and stood at its edge, looking at their shimmering images in the disturbed water. As the water quieted, the images gained in clarity and focus. After a time, they were mirrored clearly.

"Yes," she said. "A most satisfactory sight."

"I agree," he said.

"Would you hand me that bath towel, love?" she asked.

33

He moved quickly in the direction of her pointing finger, before he caught the joke. He slapped her bottom lightly and said, "You should have thought of that before you got all wet."

"Yes."

"*Now* what are you going to do?"

"I've no idea. Wait until I'm dry, I suppose."

"I know a good place to wait," he said.

"Good."

He led her through an opening in the hedge behind them to a mattress-sized, grassy knoll. Branches above formed a transparent ceiling.

"Here it is," he said.

"Yes," she said. "Here it is."

"Let's be together," he said.

And they were. Astonishingly to them both, not as tentative, apprehensive first-time partners, but as a practiced, confident, exchanging pair.

"Never before," she said, looking at him and the sky.

"Nor I," he said.

"Perfection," she whispered.

"Only you," he said.

Afterward, they lay together in wonder for a suspended time before rising to find their clothing and to dress.

The *ensoku*, new to him, was a surprising delight. Cups of hot soup (*miso-shiru*) from a Thermos bottle; then, out of a symmetric series of black and red lacquered boxes came *sushi* rolls, *sashimi*, pickled vegetables, and lotus root. Sauces and ginger and *tofu*. Sake, and later, tea.

He ate too much.

The day had taken on a shape and color of its own.

She lay back on the picnic blanket and said, "I am very happy."

He joined her. His arm moved, quite naturally, under her head. Her head found its place in an indentation of his shoulder. Two halves had joined to become one.

They slept. The birds and small animals which had been somewhat noisy—their privacy having been invaded and unaccustomed food brought in—grew quiet, as if respecting lovers' rights.

She awoke first, and for a minute or more, thought herself in Japan. She did not regret her error when she realized where she actually was and with whom. She turned to him and kissed him awake. He trembled, opened his eyes, and looked at her until she became real.

They repacked the picnic basket and put it into the car. They changed, pulling on bathing suits. They walked to the edge of the pond. From there, by row-boat, they made their way to the open sea. An hour of sea bathing followed in the throbbing, living waters of South Beach.

They rested on the sand and talked of pleasant things: childhood memories of summer, teachers, travel.

It was late afternoon when they returned to the car.

He led her to still another bower where love happened again as dusk fell.

After they had dressed, he brought forth his surprise: an ice bucket that held a shaker full of martinis. They sat on the running board and sipped.

"I'm *so* glad you're a pharmacist," she said.

"Are you?"

"We wouldn't have this grand medicine if you weren't."

"Sure we would. But it would be a little more illegal."

"Why is it," she asked, "that lawbreaking is so exciting?"

The question, unanswered, hung in the air.

Their talk turned now to more practical matters.

"Where shall we put the house?" he asked.

The question did not surprise her, since she had been on the verge of proposing it herself.

"I don't think we're going to be able to settle that this afternoon," she said. "This evening."

"I've often thought that hillock there," he said.

"Yes, love," she said, "that would seem the obvious place—forgive me—but there are other considerations. The direction of the prevailing winds and the sunrise-sunset positioning. The sea views, access—"

He laughed. "You're in charge, my angel. I can see I'm no match for you on this."

"What's more," she continued, warming to the subject, "the choice of an architect is vital. If it's going to be a Japanese house—"

"It is."

"—then we need a Japanese designer."

"And builder, too, don't you think?"

"Possibly," she said. "Although, if we find the right man and if he's willing to supervise, Yankee craftsmen are remarkably versatile."

"Yes, if they're willing to stop fishing long enough to work."

"They will."

After a quiet time, Freeman said, "I'll bet you don't know where the word Yankee comes from."

"No bet."

"The Dutch. They were called Jan Kees—meaning John Cheese—by the English. The way the English are called limeys and the French frogs, and so on. Then Jan Kees got to be Yankees."

Another pause.

Sheila said, "A *small* house, don't you think?"

"Yes," he agreed. "No bigger than that bower we just left. Why did we, by the way? Leave."

"It isn't going to be planned as a permanent or—a full-time residence, is it? Or is it?" she asked.

"Whatever you say."

"Well, I may change my mind, but right now I see it as a sort of hideaway—for special days—"

"Like today."

"—or weekends or holidays."

"Yes."

"The sort of place we can take care of by ourselves. So no need for anyone else around."

"And above all," he said, "no guest room."

"Agreed."

"It's going to take a long time, you know."

"How long?" she asked.

"Longer."

"Why?"

"Because some of the materials," he said, "parchments for the *shoji*, for instance—may have to be sent from Japan."

"Very well, but meanwhile why not some substitute,

some reasonable facsimile—and replace it later on? No, that's no good."

"No."

"What does it matter *how* long it takes?" she asked. "So long as we know it's going to *be?*"

"Right."

"Of course," she said, "I'll begin at once. A library. The nearest good one is Boston, I suppose. I'll go there. Tomorrow."

"Tomorrow?" he said incredulously.

"Oh," she said, coming out of her reverie. "I *am* sorry. Carried away."

"We're going to have tomorrow here," he said. "I can't tell you how important it is. I've got to prove to myself that I'm alive and not dead; awake and not asleep. This is all—well, hard for me to believe."

"Believe it, my love," she said. "Believe."

VIII

THE SECOND DAY AT THE POND was much like the first, except that it began earlier and ended later. The picnic prepared by Freeman was strictly New England, rather than Japanese: deviled eggs, cold lobster mayonnaise, cucumber and tomato salad, cold fried chicken, chow-chow, coleslaw, preserved strawberries, and homemade banana ice cream. He had cranked the White Mountain Freezer himself that morning.

38

They ate and swam and bathed and slept and loved and walked and planned.

A site for the Japanese house was enthusiastically agreed upon.

Sheila had brought a few of her cameras and used up a dozen rolls of film.

Afterward, over cocktails (whiskey sours made from his store of medicinal Old Crow bourbon), he said, "I think you *should* go in to Boston tomorrow."

She was stunned. "Do you?"

"Yes," he said. "And I'll go with you."

She frowned. "Is that wise?"

"Maybe not. But essential."

"This is a *very* small town, love," she reminded him. "We're—all of us, each of us—conspicuous."

"I'm in and out all the time," he said nervously. "Anyway. I don't care."

She looked off into the distance, as though looking into time to come. "You'll *have* to care. We both will, if we're to survive. We must be discreet."

"Fine," he said. "We'll be discreet in Boston."

She took a suite at the newly opened Ritz-Carlton Hotel, overlooking the Public Gardens.

He was assigned to a room on the floor above.

They spent two days in Boston: mornings at the Public Library in the architectural section, copying out plans and details of Japanese houses, and in the magazine section poring over *National Geographics*. A meeting with the Japanese consul general for information as to imports and the possibility of available material in the United States. They found that it was possible to ac-

39

quire certain of the needed supplies from time to time through a trading company in San Francisco called the Rising Sun Wood and Bamboo Company. Lunch the first day at Durgin-Park's in Faneuil Hall market and the second day at Locke-Ober's. Afternoons at the museums, looking for Japanese effects: the Museum of Fine Arts, the Gardner, and, in Cambridge, the Huntington, and a too-swift walk through the astonishing glass flower collection at the Agassiz Museum. They had their first dinner in the Ritz dining room; their second was a sea-food feast at the Union Oyster House. At the Plymouth Theatre they reveled in the celebrated Winthrop Ames production of *The Pirates Of Penzance*. It put them in the mood for a two-hour walk before returning to the hotel and to bed.

The second night found them at the Beacon Theatre, fascinated by an innovation: The Vitaphone (films with *sound!*), starring Marion Talley, Giovanni Martinelli and Mischa Elman. The feature film was John Barrymore in *Don Juan*.

They walked to Chinatown, had supper, took a taxi back to the Ritz, went to bed, and did not sleep until dawn.

By noon, they were on the road, heading for the Island. Having had a late breakfast of codfish cakes, they skipped lunch and went directly to the pond. There, sketches and notes in hand, their plans moved closer to realization.

After love, they sat in the car.

He took her hand and said, "I think the house is going to come right, all right. Seems to me it's well on its way. But what about us?"

"Oh, yes," she said. "I wish we could be arranged with blueprints and specifications, too."

"Maybe we can be."

"The others involved. We ought to—we have to consider them. Must."

"I don't anticipate much trouble at my end. We've been living out a mistake, being good sports about it. She'll be relieved, I'm sure."

"But Thomas, you see, is in public life, and that means—"

"Have you ever called him Tom?"

"No, I don't think so. Why?"

"Nothing. I just wondered."

"I can't do anything to hurt his career, his future. He's been utterly kind and generous always. He's a *fine* man—could be, perhaps, a great one in the right circumstances. He's devoted to his work, to public service—he really does want the greatest good for the greatest number. He lies awake nights—sometimes he paces—trying to devise means to that end. He's not personally ambitious—doesn't want power for himself—it frightens him, actually—but only to use for what he thinks right and good."

He regarded her carefully. "I think you love him," he said.

"Yes, I do," she said, "in a way. With that part of love that's respect and admiration—reverence, even. But we are not *in* love. I see now that we never were."

"Why now?"

"Because of you and me."

"Yes."

"I'm selfish, of course. I suppose we all are, to some

41

degree. But I couldn't—wouldn't—do anything that would damage him in any way." She smiled. "But then, *that's* selfish, too—because I wouldn't want to live with a burden of guilt."

"What are we going to do, then?"

"I don't know. For now, for today and tomorrow, nothing. Wait and see."

"Wait and see," he said. "That's not much of a life, is it?"

"Depends what you see after the wait," she said.

They returned to Edgartown in the darkness. He drove slowly, his left hand on the wheel, his right holding her hand tightly, desperately.

I X

SHE DID NOT TURN UP the following morning, which surprised him. He had expected her.

He spent the better part of the day composing a letter to his wife. In its final form, after a number of false starts and many drafts, it read:

June 6, 1927

My dear Colette,

I hope this letter will not be as painful for you to read as it is for me to write, but we are two adults and as such should have learned the necessity of facing facts and dealing with them honestly, especially when a situation goes beyond the simple method of "living with it."

Our marriage is a failure, as witness how little we share

it. Maybe "failure" is the wrong word. Our marriage is simply useless. What does either of us derive from it in the way of comfort or joy or practical application? This is only one of the many, many questions I have been asking myself for the past few years. I have no doubt that you have questions, as well.

You never liked it here on the Island and from the beginning made me feel that I had somehow betrayed you by extolling its virtues. But, believe me, I did not mean to deceive you. When I told you about this place I love, I described it as it seems to me.

Could you have *learned* to love it more, to become a part of it? There's another question and one to which I do not have the answer. But what could I have done or—to put it more to the point—what can I do now? This is where my life is and my business and my work and, I suppose, my future. At thirty-four, I can hardly be expected to pull up roots and begin again elsewhere.

On the other side of the coin, there is your problem of displacement. You seem to have solved it—at least in part—by your trips. Are you aware of the fact that they have become longer and longer? And of the harmful effect they may be having on Jacqueline? I say nothing, you will note, about their effect on me.

But this brings us to our daughter, the one beautiful thing we have created together—and the one who must be considered first and above all. We are responsible to her and for her. I am perfectly prepared to assume the task of her upbringing, since it is no secret (between us) that I was the one who wanted her to begin with.

Further, since you are only thirty-one and extremely attractive and charming—I have no doubt that a more suitable marriage partner will be forthcoming. It might be best, therefore, from your point of view, to be unencumbered.

Needless to say, I am grieved about all this. It has lain between us, unspoken, for so long. I wish I had found a way to say it earlier. I have a strong suspicion that you have probably been undergoing a similar struggle.

My dear Colette, I am so sorry to have failed you. I beg your forgiveness. I bear no malice, no ill-feeling, no bitterness—only a deep sense of disappointment.

Please let me hear from you as soon as possible.

Kiss Jacqueline and tell her I am sending her a picture letter later today.

In all sincerity,
Freeman

Toward the end of the day, Sheila came into the shop. She browsed until all the customers had left, then sat up at the soda fountain and ordered an orangeade.

As Freeman prepared it, she said, "A change in plans. We're leaving for Washington day after tomorrow."

He stood still for a few seconds before continuing his work.

"I see," he said.

"We hope to be back—perhaps more than once—before the end of summer."

"Tomorrow?" he asked.

"Impossible."

He served the orangeade. She drank it. He watched her. She paid and left.

Early in the morning, on the day of her departure, she came to the back door of the store, knocked, and entered the office.

They embraced powerfully.

44

"I haven't much time," she said.

They sat down to talk. No coffee. The break in the ritual was upsetting to them both.

"I've written a letter," he said and showed her a copy. She read it, nodded, and handed it back.

"Have *you* done anything?" he asked.

"Yes. Quarreled."

"What was it about?"

"Nothing—like most quarrels," she said. "Arrangements. He sensed that I don't want to leave—he's extremely sensitive—and it irritated him. It led to words and, of course, we each said far more than we meant to say."

"We're *never* going to quarrel. I'll see to it."

"Poor man," she said, looking out the window. "He's under a great strain. This last trip. And the one just ahead."

"Something gone wrong?"

"No. The opposite."

"I don't follow," said Freeman.

"He's accustomed to things going wrong. It's part of his profession. He once said to me, 'Every day, usually at breakfast, I estimate the number of things that are probably going to go wrong in the course of the day. Fifty-five. A hundred and two. Thirty. Then, if it turns out to be only fifty-two or a hundred and one or twenty, I'm ahead of the game.'"

"He sounds wise."

"He is. And more. No, this time, his anxiety's caused by the fact of this new appointment being discussed. A great promotion. Enormous responsibility. He honestly doesn't believe he's up to it. He's said so to President

Coolidge, but the President, being a New Englander, thinks people can do anything they put their minds to."

"He may be right," said Freeman.

"So Thomas is torn between his own misgivings—he's truly modest—and his wish to serve."

"Can you tell me what it is? The appointment?"

"No. I can't."

"Sorry. Is it something that would take you away somewhere?"

She touched him and said, "I can't tell you that, either. Not yet."

"When might you know?"

"In a few weeks, I should think."

"And meanwhile—Washington?"

"Yes," she said.

"Hot there just now, isn't it?"

"Yes. A most unfortunate climate."

"May I write to you?"

"I want to say yes, but I'm afraid it would be foolish."

"A post office box?" he suggested tentatively.

She thought it over.

"I suppose so—if—. No. Better not. It would mean going there and—well, Washington."

"The telephone? Any way? I have a private line here."

He jotted down the number and gave it to her.

"Of course, I'll try," she said. "If only to keep you informed."

She glanced at the clock which had begun to hammer away the time with ear-splitting loudness.

"I must go," she said.

46

"Well," he said and took her shoulders. "These days. Our days. They've been the best I've ever known. I have no words to—." His eyes filled with tears. "I love you," he said. "Now. Always. Whatever."

"We share love," she said.

He kissed her with gentleness, but with deep feeling that echoed the passion of their recent time together.

She was gone. He went to work.

X

COLETTE'S REPLY TO HIS LETTER was her reappearance three and a half weeks later.

That afternoon, Sheila had telephoned him to say that Thomas Van Anda had accepted the appointment. He was now roving ambassador with an executive commission. He was to travel to the principal United States embassies throughout the world and prepare a report on each for the President and the Secretary of State. It would take two years, perhaps longer. There might be periodic returns to the States, but this was by no means certain.

Freeman had spent the rest of the day attempting to come to grips with the shattering reality of the situation. He had walked to the lighthouse at Starbuck Neck and beyond. He had talked to a dog. He had talked to himself.

He had closed the store at 9:30 P.M. As the evening was cool, with a southwest breeze moving across the Is-

47

land, he had decided to walk again, taking a long route home.

As he approached his house on Cooke Street, he saw that lights were on throughout. He could not imagine how or why. Mrs. Tremaine came three times a week to look after the house, but this was not one of the days.

As he went into the living room, he was startled to find his wife sitting there. She was still in her traveling clothes, including hat and gloves. She appeared to be on the verge of leaving, although he knew that she had just arrived.

"Colette!" he exclaimed and moved toward her. As he bent down to kiss her, she turned her head away. He stepped back, saw that her eyes were blazing.

"Where's Jacqueline?" he asked. "Asleep?"

"She is home," replied Colette. "In Marne-La-Co-quette."

Freeman's attempt to control his anger made his heart pound.

"You left the child *behind?* Alone?"

"She is not alone," said Colette tightly. "It is better for her there—not here with a father who wishes to break his home."

"I hoped," he said quietly, "that after all these years—"

"You shall not have one divorce. Never! I have come now only to leave you for all. But divorce? You will see me dead or I will see you dead. I am no foolish American wife without spirit. You wish to exchange me for something better—someone—as you do your automobiles, you Americans. I am no machine, you hear? I *hate* you! She will not have you—*who* she is!"

48

"Don't be ridiculous, Colette. Of course there's no one else."

"Liar!" she screamed.

He felt himself blush as he continued. "Good God! Wouldn't I have told you if it was a question of—"

"I am not fooled," she said. "There has been talk—much talk—in this dirty little village—you believe I am with no one here, but I have friends."

"Friends!" he said bitterly and wondered if indeed some word might have come to her. How? "Colette, I swear to you—"

"*Cochon!*" she screamed and rushed from the room. Sobs overtook her halfway up the stairs. She sank down and wept.

Freeman moved to her. She struck out at him with her handbag, pulled herself to her feet, and made her way upstairs. A door slammed. The wall brackets trembled.

Freeman left the house and walked again.

XI

COLETTE DID NOT LEAVE, after all. The storm passed. Life fell into its old pattern of resignation.

Jacqueline was brought home by Colette's widowed sister, who stayed through the summer.

Freeman spent more and more time in his office at the back of the store. His mornings were devoted to business matters and to reading; his nights, to research.

For almost a year, he worked on a cold cure. It came to nothing more than a substance that might provide symptomatic relief. There were plenty of those on his shelves now, he concluded, and abandoned the project.

He returned to his efforts to develop an insect repellent. Although he did not succeed, the work itself provided a needed distraction.

Some evenings, after the store had been closed, he pursued the dream of the Japanese house. He was in correspondence with Japanese architects in various parts of the United States as well as several in Japan. He kept three filing drawers: Interior, Exterior, Gardens.

This, research experiments, his daughter, and his love became, as years passed, the four corners of his existence.

With Jacqueline, he fished and sailed and talked. Like most of the Island children, she was an expert sailor, moving steadily from catboat, to starfish, to sailboat, to yawl. She raced, often won; swam and dived. She grew to be beautiful and became increasingly eager to get away from the unspoken tension of her home.

Sheila and Freeman met only twice in the first two years following her departure.

Once, during a weekend when she and her husband came to visit Island friends, eight months after Thomas had undertaken his new assignment.

She and Freeman went to the pond in separate cars as dusk fell one evening.

It was as though they had been separated for no more than a day or two. They were together.

He told her of Colette's continuing inflexible position.

"It doesn't matter," said Sheila. "Our time will come."

"When?"

She told him then of further complications. Her husband, working feverishly, had made a brilliant success of his job. As a result of this, there was talk now of a Cabinet appointment in the event that Herbert Hoover were to be elected.

"But that'd mean Washington, wouldn't it?" said Freeman.

"Yes, love. But—"

"But what?"

"The Cabinet. Time. It all gets more and more—." She stopped as her voice caught.

Freeman reached over and took her hand.

He had brought along some of the newer plans for the house. They were discussed as though realization was imminent.

Sheila and Freeman parted, more secure in their love than ever before—and more determined to be patient and discreet, to behave well.

Another year was to pass before their next encounter. New York this time. Three days at the St. Regis, never leaving her suite.

Herbert Clark Hoover had become President of the United States. Thomas Van Anda had joined his cabinet.

Van Anda's considerable assets were placed, as was customary, in a holding trusteeship in order to avoid any possible conflict of interest.

Within the year, the historic stock market collapse occurred. Technicalities made it impossible for Thomas

Van Anda to deal with his securities. He was sold out and informed, over the telephone, one October morning, that he was bankrupt.

Sheila took the news stoically and well, but within a month Thomas suffered the first of a series of heart attacks that were to incapacitate him for a decade.

They returned to New York. Sheila went to work as a salesclerk in the book department at R. H. Macy and Co. She had not been able to turn her skill in photography into a means of livelihood, since the craft was greatly overcrowded. Later, she found more lucrative employment in various publishing houses and by 1939 had become the East Coast story editor for the Universal Pictures Corporation.

She and Thomas lived quietly in a cheerful, small apartment on Riverside Drive. It was a fortunate location for a semi-invalid, since the river life he could observe was endlessly fascinating.

On his so-called "good days" he tried seriously to get on with a book he had been writing for many years: a critical survey of the Foreign Service from the end of the war to the present.

It was during this time that Freeman found himself living three lives. There was the workaday one, involving the duties and responsibilities of his daily existence: bills, food, shelter, clothing; business, correspondence, news, births and deaths and marriages; dentist, doctor, lawyer; a new will to be prepared and signed; unhappy letters from Jacqueline, happy letters from Jacqueline; conferences with his wife (they no longer conversed, only conferred); plans, arrangements arrangements arrangements and the cancellation of most of them; the daily newspapers and the burgeoning radio reports that were now supplementing them; political anxieties and economic clouds. This, in essence, was one entity.

Then there was the more vivid ongoing life he lived in imagination. This one involved both the near and the infinite future, which he shared with Sheila. They traveled and worked and walked together. Japan was part of this pattern. They went each year for an indefinite stay. They had a Plan of Life in which work and development and recreation and achievement and detail were all neatly shepherded. This aspect was made partly of memory, mainly of plans.

The third of his lives was the one he had in reality with Sheila, during which his senses sharpened, his blood flowed more swiftly through his veins, and affirmation filled the surrounding air. However limited these periods, however cruelly spaced—still they represented fulfillment.

He longed for the time when the latter two would become one. There was no question in his mind that it would come, it was only a question of when.

Sheila and Freeman met infrequently, but always with joy. They were often forced to settle for odd times and curious places, but nothing seemed to matter so long as they could be together.

Their life developed, as do all lovers' lives, areas of interest, a language, private jokes, and shared subjects. Sharing was the base of their mutuality. In addition to things, they shared feelings, worries, illnesses and recoveries, angers and ecstasies.

The passionate interest in Japan was a bond from the

53

start, and as the years passed, became at times a consuming one.

She brought more music into his life: especially Mozart, Mahler, and Brahms. And Bach.

He reintroduced her to nature, on which, by and large, she had turned her back since leaving the ranch of her girlhood. Animals and weather and flowers soon returned to charm and inspire her again. They avoided zoos and circuses, but sought out wildlife sanctuaries.

Their main topic, however, was the developing human species, particularly as it could be observed by a careful study of unique individuals—those who broke out of the ranks from time to time—to sing new songs or fight new battles.

Gertrude Stein, whom Sheila had met several times in Paris, interested her. Alexis Carrel—mainly as a nutritionist—fascinated him. They read Gustav Eckstein's *Canary* aloud, alternating chapters, and followed his work from then on, delighted at being taken so intimately into the world of birds and animals and insects and the human body.

Their life together was rich, richer.

"Did I ever tell you about General Nagaoka?" she asked one night.

"Who?"

"The man with the great mustache?"

"If you did, I forgot."

"Oh, no," she said. "You'd *never* forget this."

"Forget what?"

"The mustache. It was two feet long."

"Did you say *two feet?*"

54

"One foot from here to here," she demonstrated. "The other, here to here. It was truly resplendent—white, when I finally got to see it in the flesh."

"In the hair, you mean."

"Yes, I suppose I do. He was a distinguished man, really, aside from his oddity. Headed the Japanese Air Force, I believe. And at one time, it was quite the thing to be photographed with him—in the way one is with the Leaning Tower in Pisa. And we were—Thomas and I. I have the photograph still. Well. Listen to this. A letter from my friend Iwasa Ito—now I *have* told you about *him*."

"The innkeeper."

"Son of," she said. "Here's his letter. 'Most Honored of Friends . . .'—oh, I can skip some of this—and then —here. 'You shall be interested to hear of the death of our old General Gaishi Nagaoka because of kidney. An ancient of seventy-five and doubtless you are remembered of his outstanding growth of mustache—precisely one third of his own full height. Before his immolation, at his instruction, came his eldest son, cut off mustaches. Same were wrapped then in finest white burial silk, placed upon cushion of satin which, in turn, placed in casket of its own and buried with honor. Not cremation as was man to whom belonged these celestial mustaches . . .' And then it goes on. Isn't that a splendid account?"

Freeman was regarding her.

"You look eleven years old," he said. "I could get arrested."

XII

IN LATER YEARS, they relaxed discretion and began to exchange letters. Hers were sent to the store, his to her office. The letters were no more than friendly, yet Sheila and Freeman learned to read feeling into simple announcements.

He once wrote:

Jacqueline is in love. She has not said so, but I see her smiling secretly to herself; she cries at Brahms; she is reading Edna St. Vincent Millay. First love. Is there anything sweeter? Yes. In France, when they say, "*Si jeunesse savait . . . ,*" the rest is implied, meaning, "If youth knew; if age could!" But then, as you know, I am not greatly in sympathy with the philosophy of the French!

On another occasion, in a letter of hers:

Thomas's bad days are beginning to outnumber his good days. He is extremely patient (I am not!) and courageous and more understanding. We had planned a weekend in Old Lyme with friends recently. At the last moment he informed me that he was simply not up to it. I'm afraid I behaved less than gracefully. When he begged me to go out somewhere by myself, I did. I called several friends (some of them long-distance), but could find no one. What do you think I did? You'll never guess! I went to three movies. Yes. Three! In one day. "The Grapes of Wrath" (well made and moving, but no match for the stupendous book); "Pinocchio" (turned me into a child—a *terrified* child); "The Westerner" (you may consider Mr. Cooper a Hated Rival!). All this and phoning Thomas in between, of course. Imagine it. A day and part of an evening spent sitting in the dark and watching other people's dreams! What am I coming to?

FREEMAN to SHEILA:

Still another birthday. They seem to come and go more swiftly these days. This one was distinguished by the fact that it went unnoticed by all—wife, daughter, you. I thank you for forgetting, but I resent them. They owe me—well, at least, a Woolworth card.

What an odd factor is time! Here I am—getting on, as they say—yet younger than I have been since the days when I was one of the basketball heroes at the Edgartown High School.

You have done this, my love. You have given me youth. Shall we call it your birthday gift to me? Yes. Thank you.

I feel young, I am healthy and reasonably happy and—oh God!—how impatient.

Yours,
F.

SHEILA to FREEMAN:

Dearest, I make lists. Questions I want to ask you. Things I want to tell you. Places we must visit together. Activities in which we are to engage. The agenda grows longer and longer. Will we have time for it all? I get scared sometimes. Am I hoping for more than is possible? No. Life—our sort of life—is limitless, isn't it? Tell me that it is. You have so enriched me in so many ways. I see and hear and touch and smell and taste so much more vividly since you. Since us. Yet I only half enjoy these new-found sensitivities. I need you near to share them. How often I think, "He

would like this." "He would laugh." "I wonder what he—"
I wonder. I wonder. Please know that you are with me
always. I thank you for removing loneliness from my life.
You have given me so many lovely memories. You provide
so much to hope for. I do not send you my love because
you already have it. Keep it safe, my darling, as I do yours.
Deep inside me, warming me always.

S.

XIII

WHEN, IN 1941, Pearl Harbor was bombed and,
the following day, war declared, Thomas Van Anda
flew to Washington and volunteered his services to the
Secretary of State. Republicans and Democrats were
forming a wartime coalition. People were extending
themselves. Van Anda put his illness aside.

He was asked if he would accept a post in London,
where diplomats with organizational abilities and experience were much needed. He accepted with a single
provision: that his wife be given employment in the
same area. Granted.

Sheila and Freeman had a day together before she
flew to London via Air Transport Command.

He told her that he had called the Naval Recruiting
Office in Boston to discuss possible service. He was told
that there might be something despite his age—forty-
eight. Qualified pharmacists were at a premium. In all

likelihood, he would be sent to the Pacific to fight his second war.

Their own problems seemed infinitesimal on this day when the world seemed to be on the verge of destruction.

Their farewell was purposeful and austere.

Ten months later, through a series of curious coincidences and one classification error, Freeman found himself on his way to London to take part in the preparations for Operation Overlord. The naval officer who had been assigned to head the Pharmaceutical Unit had proved to be not a pharmacist but a farmer. Freeman, as a Chief Petty Officer in training for duty in the Pacific, was swiftly located, commissioned Commander, and flown to England.

He telephoned Sheila from London Airport. She was working in the Publications Division of the O.W.I. and living, thanks to the friendship of a British author she had once edited, in one of the charming flats at Albany, just off Piccadilly.

She was not in her office, but a secretary, responding to the urgency in Freeman's voice, gave him Sheila's home number.

Thomas Van Anda answered and Freeman found himself unable to speak.

Meanwhile: "Hello . . . Yes? . . . *Hello!* Are you there?"

At length: "Hello. This is Freeman Osborn. I'm sorry. These phones are new to me."

"Osborn?"

"Edgartown?"

"Osborn! Good Lord. What are *you* doing here?"

"I'm in the Navy, I think."

"You think?"

"Well, to tell you the truth, it's all happened so suddenly, I haven't adjusted to it as yet. I'm a Commander."

"Already? *That* was quick."

"They needed someone to run a pharmacy and that's what I do."

"Of course."

"Theirs is bigger than mine, but I'll manage, I guess," said Freeman, trembling.

"Congratulations."

"And how are you? Both."

"Hectic," said Van Anda. "Along with the rest. You must come in for a drink one day."

"Thank you. Whenever you say."

"No. Whenever Mrs. Van Anda says. She runs this place. Drop her a note and tell her where you are, won't you?"

"Certainly."

"She's out shopping somewhere. Fortnum and Mason's, probably." He laughed. "She's never out of the bloody place. The other day, I accused her of taking this flat mainly because it's right across the street from Fortnum's—and she didn't deny it!"

"Is that so?"

"God knows, there's hardly any other reason to live here. It's three hundred years old, and rickety, and if one of those things they keep dropping happens to fall within half a mile—we'll have *had* it, as they say here."

"Well," said Freeman, "let's hope there's—"

"Good of you to call," said Van Anda. "Goodbye."

Freeman found a taxi, threw his gear (duffle bag,

Valpac, footlocker, and flight bag) into the front; got into the back and said, "Fortnum and Mason's, please."

"Fortnum and bloody Mason's, did you say, mate?"

"Yes."

"Are you *sure?* It's a shop, y'know, not a hotel."

"Yes."

"Right, then."

They drove off. Freeman had not seen England in three years, and as he observed the passing scenes, he became aware of how much it had changed. The great, floating barrage balloons that circumscribed the city gave it a carnival air and served to point up, in contrast, the drab city. More bicycles than he had ever seen before. Uniforms everywhere. The inevitable trench coats, mostly soiled. Yet he sensed (could he be imagining it?) a fierce determination in the atmosphere.

"How's it going?" he asked the greasy-capped driver.

No answer.

He leaned forward and tried again. "How's it all going?"

The cabby, staring straight ahead, said, "Loose lips sink ships."

"Look, ol' fella," said Freeman, bristling, "this may come as a surprise to you—but we *are* on the same side."

"I've got me orders, mate," said the cabby tightly. "Same as you."

"Well, I'll be damned."

"What was that?"

"You're the first ally I've run into. I must say, it's one hell of a reception."

"Sorry. We're too busy to call out the blinkin' Coldstream Guards for every Yank turns up, y'know. And we're tired, some of us. We've been at it, y'know, for two years an' more."

Freeman leaned back and reasoned that he had simply struck a disagreeable, recalcitrant man. He cautioned himself to form no judgments on the basis of a single encounter. Still, he could not resist asking. "But what have *you* got against *me?*"

"You—me? Nothing, personally. But what our *chaps*'ve got against the Yanks, they say, is: 'They're overpaid, oversexed, and over *here!*' "

Freeman laughed, the ridiculous wheeze bringing him out of his gloom. The cabby joined him and, all at once, they were friends.

In front of Fortnum and Mason's, Freeman swiftly negotiated a waiting price, and the knowing cabby arranged to pick him up at the rear entrance.

"Bottom of Jermyn Street," he said. "By the way, if y'want a smashin' place to get your hair cut, I recommend Laurie and Jones, right down the street there. Chums of mine, they are. And real artists. They look after a lot of the best of the stage people."

"Thanks. I'll remember that."

He moved into the elegance of Fortnum's and was struck at once by the continuing sense of custom and tradition. Out in the streets, World War II stamped everyone and everything; in this shop, the world was as it had ever been: the morning-coated floorwalkers, the formal clerks, the gracious service.

Freeman searched for his love, thought once he saw her in the distance, rushed to the spot, found he was wrong. He was reluctant to leave, convinced that she was under this roof or, if not, would be at any moment.

But after half an hour of fruitless exploration, and noting that one of the floorwalkers was beginning to regard him suspiciously, he made a purchase (tea biscuits), went once more through the store, left, and found his taxi.

His billet was a pleasant two-room flat in Knightsbridge, a short walk to the Naval Supply Depot where he was to make his headquarters.

He unpacked, slept for an hour, and went to the naval officers' mess for dinner. The food was plentiful and surprisingly good. He walked, finding his way to Piccadilly and to the Albany gate. He traversed the block containing its driveway entrance. Back and forth, back and forth, until the aggressive streetwalkers who frequented the area began to mistake him for a potential client. When they became too importunate, he moved on to Piccadilly Circus, Leicester Square, Trafalgar Square.

Night fell quickly and he was confronted with the phenomenon of the blackout for the first time. Despite his recent training and briefing, he was unprepared for the aspect of a city truly in total darkness; traffic crawling, people bumping into one another. He was determined to find his way home. It took him just under three hours.

The night that followed alternated between deep sleep and intense wakefulness. The sleep was dreamless, but the wakefulness was filled with visions of what might be expected in the months to come.

The whims of war had brought them to the same place, but how could they, how would they manage a life?

The billet itself was hopeless, a noisy hutch. Would he be permitted to move—assuming he could find a place? A different flat? A large hotel? A small one? A place in the country? Idyllic images came to an abrupt end as the impracticability of his ideas struck him.

He was asleep again.

In the morning, he reported to his station and was swept without delay into the infinitely complex world of D-Day preparation. He forgot to lunch and it was not until the afternoon tea break that he found himself free to call Sheila.

She was not in, a secretary informed him.

"Can you tell me where I might reach her? It's rather urgent. A personal matter. I'm a friend of hers. Commander Osborn."

"Yes, I know."

"You do?"

"As a matter of fact," she said, "I've been trying to track you down all day, but your Navy hasn't been helpful, I *must* say."

He gave her his addresses and phone numbers, then said, "And you're sure there's no place I can reach her now?"

"Well, yes—no, I think not."

"What?"

"Actually, she's gone to the doctor's and I don't think she's—"

"Is she ill?"

"I'm sure I don't know, sir. Please don't ask me any more. I'm quite flustered."

He hung up and worried.

At five o'clock, when his duties for the day had

been completed, he went by taxi to Fortnum and Mason's again. He could think of nothing else to do, having rejected the thought of calling her office again as well as the idea of trying her at home. Either move, he considered, would be less than prudent.

He wandered about the shop, aimlessly, only half searching, since his reason told him that her presence there was most unlikely.

At the back of the shop, as he stood looking at a shelf of tinned goods from Portugal, an unmistakable scent hit his nostrils with the force of a punch in the nose. He whirled about.

There, on a high stool at the service counter, he saw a familiar back and the bun of hair so dear to him. Sheila. Sheila. He moved toward her at once, but stopped as he saw that she was in conversation with a handsome man. He knew the face, but it took him a long moment to place it. Of course. Edward R. Murrow. He began to walk away, could not bear the direction, turned again and approached the couple. "Excuse me."

"Freeman!" she cried and put out her hand, smiling radiantly. "This is Ed Murrow."

"Yes, I know."

"How do you do, Commander?"

"This is a great honor, Mr. Murrow," said Freeman.

"Thank you."

"Freeman!" Sheila repeated. "Of all people! I'd ask you to join us, but we're deep in business. I'm trying all my charms and wiles on this man to make him do something for me, but so far they're not working. And I'm running out of charm!"

65

"They're working," said Murrow. "And pretty soon, *I'll* be working. Harder than I like."

Sheila regarded Freeman, her face flushed. "I *am* surprised to see you. But aren't you supposed to be in the Pacific?"

"Diverted," said Freeman.

"I'm *so* glad," she said. "This seems to be a *much* better war. Thomas mumbled something about a call from you, but he's so vague these days, I couldn't be certain. I asked the office to check and they reported you as nonexistent."

"I am, most of the time."

"Now, now. None of that. You're doing very well. A commander! Think of it."

"Yes. Well, they don't let me command much. My title ought to be comman*dee*, I think."

A pause. Freeman knew that he must leave, yet he waited.

"Look here," Sheila said suddenly. "I'm meeting Thomas in about half an hour. Please come. He'd be *so* delighted to see you."

Freeman demurred. "Well—"

"*Please!*" she said, and it struck him that she was attempting communication on another level. "We're meeting at the Cavendish. Do you know where it is?"

"No."

"Well, it's right there," she pointed. "Out that door and across the street. Half an hour. In the bar. If I'm a few minutes late—it all depends on this difficult man— talk to Thomas. He's longing to see you."

"All right. Pleased to have met you, Mr. Murrow."

"Goodbye," said Murrow.

66

They shook hands. Sheila turned away. Freeman left.

He located the Cavendish Hotel, a small establishment in Jermyn Street, and walked about, trying to unravel his tangled information.

What did she mean—"He's longing to see you."? Of course. That meant he would not be there at all! This notion was confirmed by: "If I'm late, talk to him."

Half an hour. He looked at his watch. Walked faster. Saw a small sign in the window of a hatter's shop: "Laurie and Jones." He knew those names. How? It took him five minutes to recall the cabby's recommendation.

He went to the Cavendish bar and ordered a scotch and water.

"Out, I'm afraid," said the waitress.

"What *do* you have?"

"Du-*bonny*, pink gin, vermouth, and—"

"That'll do. Pink gin."

He wondered what it was and was beginning to find out when Sheila arrived. He rose. She joined him and ordered.

"Same for me, please." Then loudly, looking about, "Thomas not here yet?"

"No."

"That man is *never* on time."

Freeman spoke softly. "Is he coming at all?"

"No," she said quietly. "Of course not. He's in conferences tonight."

Her drink was served. They raised their glasses to each other.

"Cheers," he said. "Isn't that what we say over here?"

"Cheers," she said.

"Why the doctor?" Freeman asked.

"What?"

"Why did you have to see the doctor?" he insisted.

Sheila blinked. "I'll kill that girl," she said.

"My fault," he said. "I tricked her into telling me. I was desperate to find you."

"All right, then. I *won't* kill her."

"Now," he said. "Why the doctor?"

"I'm overweight. You must see it."

"Yes, I do," he said.

"You're supposed to say, 'No, I don't.'"

"No, I don't," he said.

"Or else, 'Yes, but it's *so* becoming.'"

"Yes," he said, "but it's *so* becoming."

"If I'd known about you turning up, I wouldn't have let it happen. I'm sorry."

"It doesn't matter," he said.

"It matters to me."

He finished his drink, signaled the waitress, and asked Sheila, "Would you like another?"

"No, thank you," she replied. "I just went on a strict diet."

"One more for me," he said to the waitress.

"With pleasure, sir. The lady?"

"Nothing, thank you," said Sheila.

Freeman took a deep breath, relaxed, and looked about.

"What a nice place," he said.

"I'm *so* glad you like it," she said over the rim of her glass, "because you live here."

"I do?"

"Yes," she replied and handed him a key. "In four-

68

oh-five. It's what they call a bed-sitter." She turned Cockney and added, "*Evah* so noice!"

"Have I been in it long?"

"Only since this morning. A lad from my office brought your bags over and checked you in."

The waitress served Freeman his second pink gin.

"Thank you," he said.

Sheila spoke to the waitress. "Would you ask the hall porter if he could spare us a moment?"

"Certainly, madame."

Sheila and Freeman exchanged a long look.

"He needs your passport—or documents—whatever," she said. "Just for an hour or so."

Freeman shook his head slowly and contemplated her with wonder.

"Sheila, Sheila, Sheila," he said.

The hall porter took his military passport and welcomed him.

A few minutes later, Freeman said goodbye to Sheila at the door and went up to 405. There he found the most pleasant of rooms: old, but beautifully appointed. It was on the back, quiet, and overlooked a mews.

There were flowers in the room, a basket of fruit, a tray of drinks. There were American magazines and a stack of paperbacks from the American Forces Library and a copy of the *Vineyard Gazette*. This last item told him who had arranged the room.

The bags—not his—had been unpacked. Uniforms hung in the closet, shirts and socks, pajamas and underwear had been put away, toilet articles arranged.

A knock at the door. He opened it. Sheila came in.

69

He closed the door and locked it as she went to the windows and drew the blinds.

They moved toward each other and touched.

"Welcome home, my darling," she said.

"Thank you," he whispered. "Thank you for everything. For my life."

There were no further words, not for a long, loving time.

They sat, she in a man's dressing gown, he in his raincoat, each eating a piece of fruit.

"Darling?" she asked. "What is chlo*restol*?"

"You probably mean 'cholesterol.'"

"Probably."

"I can tell you," he said. "It may take awhile—but why do you want to know?"

"Because I've got it," she said.

"*Everyone's* got it, you goose."

"Then why's the doctor so frowny about it?"

"Maybe you have too much. Then it's a problem."

"Serious?"

"Not very, no," he said. "A question of diet, that's all."

"Isn't there a medicine? I'm sure he mentioned something."

"Yes, but we're not going to take it," he said.

"Why not?"

"Well, it's still in the experimental stage, and I don't want my girl to be a guinea pig."

"I'm not your girl."

"Of course you are."

"I'm your mistress."

"All right."

"I *love* being your mistress."

"I think you're going to love being my wife even more."

"I wonder." She smiled. "Odd. When I am, I'll be Mrs. Osborn, won't I? M-r-s."

"Yes."

"Well, doesn't that stand for 'mistress'?"

"Does it?"

"Of course. I'll simply be changing from mistress to Mistress. Small m to big M is about the only difference."

"Well, I told you in the beginning—didn't I?—that there wasn't much chance for advancement in this line of work."

"No, you didn't," she said.

"Didn't what?"

"Tell me any such thing."

"I should have."

They went back to bed. Lying in each other's arms, he caressed her. The caresses became an examination.

"I don't feel any cholesterol," he said.

"What is it? You were going to tell me what it is."

He explained, in full physiological detail. Sheila listened with interest.

"What it comes down to, then," she said finally, "is that I eat too much."

"Too much of what's wrong."

"Yes. I always do when I'm unhappy. Discontented. Unsatisfied."

"We all do. It's the quick and easy answer."

"You should have seen me as a high school girl. Sulky and roly-poly."

"Come here."

So began their war years, which, as it happened, were to be the best of their life together.

Freeman moved from his billet, and the Cavendish remained his home until four months after V-E Day.

The months to D-Day were charged with anticipatory excitement. They both felt increasingly useful in their work, and the sense of being part of a plan of high purpose was invigorating.

They began by respecting and admiring many British individuals, and ended by loving them en masse. The spirit, the will, the devotion, and, above all, the humor of the people enchanted them.

In an organizational meeting one morning, Freeman said to his British opposite number, "Well, that's something I'll have to take up with the chaplain."

"Right you are. And I'll have a go at *our* J.C.L.O."

"J.C.L.O.?" inquired Freeman.

"Why, yes," said the British major. "Jesus Christ Liaison Officer."

There were frequent separations, but Sheila and Freeman were learning to accept them as a part of their life.

Sheila's weight became one of their private, family jokes. As a rule, her weight lessened when they were together and went up when they were separated.

In time, she acquired two complete wardrobes, one for each condition.

The first time Thomas Van Anda had to return to Washington, he phoned Freeman.

"Osborn?"

"Yes?" said Freeman.

"Van Anda here."

"Yes?"

"Look here, old man. I'm off to the Z.I. for a week or two, and I wonder if you'd do me a *great* service."

"Of course. Whatever I can."

"It's only to keep an eye on Mrs. Van Anda. Could you possibly give her a ring each day and see she's all right? I don't know how you're fixed for time, but perhaps you could take her to dinner once or twice and, of course, she loves the theatre here—I can't see why, I don't get half they're saying half the time—but she dotes on it—so you might escort her if you can spare an evening. I'll want to reimburse you for all this, of course, and—"

"Oh, no."

"Now, now. I insist. Yes. Oh, and if anything should come up—problem, emergency—you can use the State Department telex. Here's my code number. Got a pencil?"

"Yes, sir."

"TVA661ST."

"I have it."

"And if you can't reach me, my secretary is Mrs. Roos. R-o-o-s."

"Is that here or there?"

"Both places. She's coming to Washington with me, of course."

"Right."

"I appreciate this, old man. She will, too. Mrs. Van Anda."

Sheila swore she had had nothing to do with the plan; that she had not engineered it directly or indirectly.

They went out nightly. The Sadler's Wells Ballet. The Old Vic. The Curzon Cinema.

Freeman could not shake his feeling of unease. In all the years of the situation, he had never felt the slightest guilt. The liaison was completely honorable, in his view. But now, to be shepherding Mrs. Van Anda about at the request of *Mr.* Van Anda was somehow embarrassing.

"He must think I'm a faggot," Freeman said to her.

"If he does," she said, "he's wrong."

"Damn! I wish he hadn't called me."

She took his arm. They were walking on the Hyde Park path beside the Ritz-Carlton, on their way to dinner.

"Love," she said, "please don't. People who live our sort of life have to make a good many compromises."

"I suppose so," he said miserably.

"It's a question of deciding whether it's worth it or not."

"It is," he said. "It's worth anything."

XIV

THOMAS VAN ANDA RETURNED from Washington.

As the great day approached, the meetings between Sheila and Freeman became less frequent.

The monumental D-Day arrow was being laboriously pulled back, back on its bowstring.

The planners began working nights and Sundays and holidays.

One evening, Freeman turned up an hour and a half late for his date with Sheila.

She was waiting for him, reading *The Go-Between* in 405, having long since acquired her own key.

He came in, clearly upset and harassed.

"Sorry, darling," he said. "It's been one of those God-damned—." He kissed her in a perfunctory, married way. She observed that a further measure of his preoccupation was the fact that he had neglected to lock the door.

She got up quickly and did it herself.

"Are you all right?" he asked automatically.

"Well, yes, considering I gave birth this morning."

"Yuh," he said.

"Twins, in fact," she added.

"What?" he said, startled.

"Nothing."

"What did you say about twins?"

"Twins?"

"I thought—well, never mind."

She went to him. He repeated the kiss.

"Oh, come, come," she said. "We can do better than that."

They kissed again.

She laughed and said, "Well, not *much* better."

"Are you sure," he asked, "you didn't say something about twins?"

"Yes."

"A word like it?"

He went to the tray of drinks and poured himself a

drink. He did not, as was his custom, ask her if she wanted one. Further, he had not yet removed his cap. Finally, the drink he poured was far stronger than usual. She knew that something had gone very wrong.

She pointed to the glass in his hand and asked, "Did you mean to make it as brown as that?"

"What?" he asked.

"Twins," she said.

He looked at her for a long, befuddled time, before taking a large swig of his drink.

"What is it, love?" she asked. "Tell me."

"Listen," he said. "I want to ask you something. And I want you to answer truthfully. I mean, don't say what you think *I'd* want you to say. Give me a straight answer. O.K.?"

She nodded and steeled herself for what was coming.

"Here's the question," he said.

She was ready to scream "Where?" while he took another swallow, set down his glass, took off his cap, and tossed it aside.

He took a step toward her and asked, "Would you consider toilet paper a pharmaceutical supply?"

She knew from his intensity that he was in deadly earnest, and tried to keep a straight face, but failed and laughed.

Astonished, he asked, "Why's that funny?"

"It's not," she said. "Only surprising."

"Well, *would* you?"

She thought it over and answered, "Yes."

"*Ye-es?*" he said incredulously, bending the word.

"I mean, *no*," she said in a rush.

"Come on, Sheila. This is serious."

"All right. To really give you an answer I'll have to borrow one our glandular editor-in-chief used the other day at the top of an argument. He hollered, 'Hell yes-and-no!'"

"I'll go back," said Freeman, "to your first answer. The instinctive one. You said 'Yes.'"

"Yes."

"Well, you're *wrong*. Where do you buy it? In a pharmacy? Or at the grocery store? I said to them, 'Listen, gentlemen. I've run a drugstore for twenty years and never sold so much as one single roll. So don't tell *me* it comes under the heading of pharmaceutical supplies!'"

She began to get the gist of the problem, and talked it out with him. By the time he had finished his drink, she was discussing it seriously and *he* was laughing. In time, they both saw the inherent humor. The greatest military operation in all history could not be launched until the question of who was to be responsible for the toilet paper was solved.

He explained that at the last moment he had been told that it was to be an additional job for his already dangerously overloaded unit. He had protested, and the contretemps had gone up through channels where it would be finally adjudicated by General Bradley's office.

"I don't know what I'll do if it goes against me," he said. "I swear I don't think we can handle it."

They wondered together if the people back home had any concept of what was taking shape; of the size and complexity of the operation.

As they talked, they carefully avoided the slightest

77

reference to the actual date, although each knew that they were now at D-minus 3, and each knew that the other knew.

"It's taken us four months to get the God-damned *Dramamine* question straight," he said wearily. "If it *is* straight. In the landing exercises, they were appalled at how many of the kids got seasick. It comes down to the weather. If it's bad, the percentage goes up. The hell of it is, it's only a preventive. Once they're actually sick it's too late. They think now they're going to have every kid in the boats take one. First the medics worried about it making them drowsy, but the final word is that the natural excitement is going to more than compensate. So this means needing about five times more than we had—to be made, stateside, and shipped, and distributed. It's been quite a project."

"I'm very proud of you, my love," she said.

The long wait ended. The fateful Monday morning came. The landings began.

Freeman's duties took him back and forth across the Channel almost daily. For a time, he could think of nothing but the next trip.

He and Sheila met once. He fell asleep while they were making love.

X V

THEY WERE TOGETHER when the notorious V-1 rockets made their first deadly appearance on June 13, 1944, a week after the invasion of the Continent had begun. There had been no air-raid warning, only a sudden succession of fierce explosions. Half an hour or so later, the anti-aircraft fire began, and the alert was sounded.

Sheila and Freeman dressed swiftly and went out onto the street. The mysterious bombardment was being discussed by small groups everywhere. Misinformation abounded. Rescue teams sped through the city. In the sky above, from time to time, flaming crosses could be seen. A pattern became apparent: Twenty or thirty seconds after the flame went out, an explosion would occur. Did this mean that the bomb fell straight down after extinguishing? No one knew for certain.

The anti-aircraft fire became more intense. The air-raid wardens were ordering people off the streets.

Albany was only a short distance away, but it seemed foolhardy to attempt the journey.

Sheila phoned her husband at his office.

"Are you all right?" she asked.

"So far. You?"

"Yes, but I'm afraid I can't get home."

"Where are you?"

"Leicester Square," she said and described an earlier incident. "I was at the movies, but I left when they began flashing the alert on the screen. Right across Jane Russell's chest. The boys booed."

"I should think so."

"I must say, I was the only one who *did* leave. The picture had just started."

"All right," said Van Anda. "Find a comfortable spot and sit tight until the all clear."

"What's going on?"

"I'm not sure. There've been several reports, none confirmed. In any case, we'd best not discuss it on the phone."

"Sorry," she said.

"It does seem, though, that his long-touted secret weapon has finally turned up."

"Yes. Well. Take care, dear."

"Goodbye."

She and Freeman returned to the Cavendish and went to bed, fully dressed. They clung together as the raid continued.

"Wouldn't it be awful," she said, "if this were it?"

"Don't think such things," he said. "You're poisoning the air."

"It's pretty poisoned already, wouldn't you say?"

"Shall I tell you what's going to happen?" he inquired. "Or would you like it to be a surprise?"

"No. Tell me. I *hate* surprises."

"Very well. We're going to win the war in about ten months—maybe less—then we're all going home and get ourselves rearranged right. And as soon as things have calmed down in the Pacific, we're going to Japan together. I haven't decided whether we're going to fly or go by sea from San Francisco."

She waited for a deafening burst of anti-aircraft fire to subside before she spoke.

"Why not fly one way and boat the other?"

"Perfect," he said. "We'll fly there and back by boat."

"No," she said. "Boat out and plane back."

"I can see," said Freeman, "that you're going to be

a domineering partner, and it's just lucky for you that I *like* it like that."

An explosion shook the room.

"On second thought," she said, "we'll go by sea both ways. We'll make love and eat *sashimi* and study Japanese all the way there."

"And the same coming back."

"No. Sorry. Coming back, we'll be planning the house."

"Of course. Stupid of me."

"Yes," she said. "It was."

This was to be their last night together for eleven months.

As the invasion thundered on, they lost contact completely. Personal communication became increasingly difficult, especially after Sheila went on detached service to the O.S.S. and security regarding the movement of intelligence personnel became critical. In any case, there was no discreet way in which Freeman could solicit information about her. He heard, accidentally, that she had been transferred to the Continent, transferred again. Somewhere. Freeman's attempts to locate her in the chaos were fruitless. It was not until three weeks after V-E Day that Freeman returned to London. He learned that Sheila was now in Paris and that her husband had gone to the Pacific two days after the German surrender.

He managed a trip to Paris. The Scribe was the headquarters for the press as well as the intelligence services and he went there at once.

He found that Sheila Van Anda was, indeed, registered, but that she was not in at the moment.

He waited, walking about the busy hotel and the surrounding streets until well after midnight. He returned to the Scribe, inquired again. She had not returned.

He went back to his own billet and slept, clothed, for a few hours. Then he walked to the Scribe. No, she was still not in. He waited until the dining room opened at 7:00 A.M. and went in.

As he was finishing his breakfast, he looked across the room and saw two portly, uniformed women sharing a table. The light in the room was poor and he could not make out if they were Americans or British or—. They laughed. One of the laughs was stunningly familiar. He got up and rushed across the room. One of the women was Sheila.

She jumped up as he approached. They embraced. She felt strange in his arms, bulky to the touch.

"You rat!" she said. "Sneaking up on a girl like that."

"I wasn't sure it was—I mean, I've never *seen* you in uniform before."

"Isn't it dashing?" she asked. "Made by Omar the Tentmaker."

She introduced him to her companion, a young Frenchwoman attached to SHAEF.

After an aimless chat, Freeman said, "Go ahead. Finish your breakfast. Sorry to have barged in."

"And finish yours," said Sheila.

He realized that he was holding his napkin in his hand.

"Yes," he said.

"And call me up sometime, won't you?"

"Sure, if I get a chance."

82

"Soon," she said meaningfully.

"All right," he said. "Soon."

Half an hour later, he phoned her room.

"Seven-oh-seven," she said. "Hurry, love."

They talked all day, loved all night.

They ate and bathed and drank at random.

They were catching up.

She was hazardously overweight now as a result of months of terror and loneliness and the recent temptations of Parisian food.

They joked about it at first. He assured her that he found her Renoir-like ampleness attractive, which was true enough. When, however, he learned that she had not had a recent cholesterol count, it troubled him.

He took her privately to a confidential clinic on the top floor of the Hotel Meurice, run for the convenience of ranking officers.

The result of the test was not encouraging. A diet and a system of exercise were prescribed.

Freeman had every intention of supervising her treatment with care, but was precipitously ordered to the Pacific. Okinawa.

XVI

WHEN THE WAR in the Pacific ended, Freeman could not resist promoting, for himself, a trip to Japan. He wandered about on invented missions for twenty days, traveling by boat, trains, army transport, and on foot. Osaka (the amazing puppet theatre). Kyoto (the temples). Kobe (the beef!). Nagoya (the Shinto shrine). Yokohama (the devastation). Sasebo (the naval base).

Despite the gaping war wounds, the numb hostility of many, and the post-defeat chaos, Freeman found Japan to be all he had dreamed and more. Moreover, he had the unmistakable impression of Sheila at his side throughout the journey.

Back on Martha's Vineyard, life went on from where it had left off four years earlier.

Colette waited long enough to attend Jacqueline's graduation from Radcliffe, and left for France immediately afterward.

Freeman and Sheila met as often as they could; on the Island, in New York, in Washington.

Sheila and her husband had, meanwhile, come to an amicable understanding with regard to their future. Their marriage—for better or worse—had clearly run its course.

The details of their separation and divorce had only to be worked out.

Freeman and Sheila, whenever they met, talked of this and of the new subject that had come into their lives: Freeman's project. In Japan, he had encountered an English-speaking chemist who had told him of his unsuccessful, lifelong attempts to compound an effective insect repellent, much needed in the Sasebo area.

Freeman, who had long been interested in the subject, had gone back to work on the problem. The store was now being effectively run by Mrs. Petschek and Martin Stein, a young Boston pharmacist. Thus, Freeman was able to devote long, concentrated periods of time in the Chilmark barn he had converted into a laboratory. He came close to the solution on several occasions, but each time there was a flaw: insufficiently long-lasting, irritating to sensitive skins, too medicinal in odor.

He thought himself close to success one windy autumn week and worked day and night, without leaving the barn. He was to meet Sheila at the St. Regis in New York soon and wanted, more than anything, to have good news for her. He wanted her to be proud of him.

XVII

HE KNOCKED SOFTLY on the door to 1103–1105. It opened. He walked into the sitting room of the suite. It was filled with the flowers he had sent. He heard the door behind him close, the bolt thrown.

He turned to find her moving toward him. He wanted to go to her, but instinctively feared the result of collision. He let her come to him.

They were lost in their kiss. His hands and fingers, as hungry as his mouth and vitals, moved over her body. It was as though he needed reassurance that she was there, real. He needed to touch her skin. He put his hands up under her blouse, then drove her skirt down from her body.

She was loosening his belt. And still they kissed. They wanted it all, at once, like greedy children. In time, they had divested themselves and each other of clothing. A moment later, they were joined; and not long after, lying on the floor, their kiss came to an end as their bodies began the ultimate exchange. Long pent-up hope was expressed, desire fulfilled. They were two who often smiled at each other during love. Now, when their union had ended—for the time being—she laughed.

"Are you laughing?" he asked.

"I think so."

"At me?"

"At everything there is," she said.

"Why?"

"I should have told you before, of course, but the fact is, you didn't give me a chance."

"Told me what?"

"That there's a bedroom here belongs to us."

"You can't mean it!" he said.

"I do."

"You mean one of those with a bed and everything?"

"*Practically* everything," she said.

"Shall we go there?"

"Certainly not," she said as she got to her feet.

"*Why* not?" he asked.

"Because the wine is in *here*," she said.

She put on a robe while he took the bottle from the cooler and uncorked it skillfully. It was a shared favorite, Pouilly Fumé, a memory of their Paris time.

While she poured, he broke the string around the suitbox he had brought in (that old standard equipment of illicit love), and put on his dressing gown.

They touched glasses.

"I love you," he said.

And she said, "I love you."

They made themselves comfortable, close to each other, on the large sofa.

"I've got a little bad news," he said.

"Oh, no."

"The formula's no good."

"Not at all?"

"It stinks. No, what I mean is, it literally smells bad. So who the hell would want it? I know *I'd* rather be bitten than shunned."

"But you said you thought the chlorophyll would—"

"I thought wrong. It's all no damned good and what burns me is three months on the wrong track."

They sipped in depressed silence.

Then she asked, "Should I phone down and cancel the bedroom? It's rather expensive."

He thought for a beat and asked, "Would they *let* us have just this room or—wait—how about giving this up and have *just* the bedroom?"

"I wouldn't," she said.

"Why not?"

"Too suspicious. And besides, *this* is the living room —and we want to *live*, don't we?"

He got up and brought the wine bottle over to provide refills.

He said, "I remember Chico Marx explaining how he couldn't afford to keep a car and a chauffeur, so—" he went into a surprisingly adept imitation: " 'I give up-a da car, an' I keep-a da chauffeur!' "

She laughed. "I remember that. Weren't they immense?"

"I'll say. The shows. I used to go again and again, when I was in college. We all did, and we'd know the routines, finally, by heart, without even trying—and at the oddest time—day, night—in canoes and locker rooms and during exams, sometimes—we'd go into them. That insanity kept us sane somehow."

"And Ed Wynn," she mused. "Willie Howard—'Comes the revolution you'll *eat* strawberries and cream, God damn it, and *like* it!'—and Clark and McCullough—"

"I didn't *get* them," he said.

"Would you like a slap?"

"I didn't," he said.

"Why not?"

"I don't know," he said. "Under my head, I suppose. And I was more a Laurel and Hardy man, then."

"So was I," she said.

"I never knew you were a *man*," he said.

"There's a lot about me you don't know," she said mysteriously.

"But I'm going to find out."

"You know what I'd do right now if I still smoked?" she asked.

"What?"

"I'd have a cigarette."

"I wish you hadn't said that," he said, pressing her to him.

"I didn't. You just thought I did."

"Because it's been on my mind. The whole idea. I'm torn. I sell them, of course, in the store. Always have.

88

And I wish I didn't. More and more we're learning the worst. Bob Nevin told me the other day that he went to a medical convention in Atlantic City—and about three thousand doctors were in the hall, about half of them smoking, when this Wydner fellow from the Sloan-Kettering here in New York got up to read his paper on the latest findings—and he showed slides and recited statistics. Bob says it took almost an hour and by the time Wydner was finished—not a single doctor in the place was smoking."

"Fascinating," she said.

"Of course, I suppose they all started again. Most of them."

"I suppose."

"But why do I *sell* the damned things and make money on them? Would I sell *any* poison just to make money? Of course, I sell a *lot* of poison, but it's by prescription."

"My love," she said, "you're a good man—the best I know—but you can't remake the race."

"I'm not as good a man as I could be. I could put up a sign: 'This store does not sell cigarettes'—and tell why."

"They'd go somewhere else for them," she said.

"Bad argument."

"Do it, then."

"Damn it. I may at that," he said.

"Why don't you?"

"Would *you* approve?"

"I'd be proud of you," she said.

They lay together for a time, in thought.

She said, "He died, didn't he?"

"Who?"

"Willie Howard."

"Yes," he said. "I think so. . . . Everyone dies. The trick is to live before you do—and not so many do that."

"Oh, please let's live," she said.

"Yes. . . . Imagine it," he said, and began to caress her, top to toe, with his fingers and lips. "Had it not been for a single particle—I might have lived and died and never known love. . . . Did I ever think it was love? I wonder. Probably not. . . . This is love. To care more for someone than for self. To live *with* someone, *in* someone else. To feel that the other half of yourself has been joined to you. . . . I revere you. . . . Here am I, a middle-aged man, catapulted back into youth. I'm old and young and in love. . . . And new feelings, never-before sensations—one I'm ashamed of—but I'll confess it. I don't want anything between us masked or hidden. I want everything in your head and heart and here—everything. Here's the confession. I've never been possessive—surely not of people—and jealousy? Well, since I'd never known it, I could afford to be smug and think of it as a base emotion—you know, Othello's occupation, not mine. . . . And then one day —no, evening—we met—and here, right on your most beautiful neck, I saw a mark—what the teenagers call 'a hickey'—at that moment, oh, how I regretted being a druggist—because every druggist knows the mark, has been asked a thousand times for something to cover it, disguise it, before the customer could go to school or home or work or whatever. And there always *was* something. . . . And, suddenly, there it was, a fire in my middle I'd never known—anger and resentment and insult—that neck belonged to *me!* How dare anyone bruise it—and, of course, other thoughts, forbidden. This is an apology. I had no right to feel any of that, think any of that."

"You are my love," she said.

XVIII

TWO MONTHS WERE TO PASS before he was able to implement his no-cigarette-sales principle. It was more complex than he had imagined. The jobber who supplied him with tobacco products handled other goods as well and, fearful that Freeman's move might encourage others, refused to sell Freeman what he wanted selectively. Freeman's trip to Boston to argue the case failed, as did his attempts to make other arrangements for his needs. A complicated, rooted, franchise system was in force.

There were further talks with Sheila, but with no one else.

At length, the sign appeared in his store.

THIS STORE, PROFESSIONALLY
CONCERNED WITH THE HEALTH
AND WELL-BEING OF THE COMMUNITY
IT SERVES, DOES NOT SELL CIGARETTES,
CIGARS, PIPE TOBACCO, TOBACCO
IN ANY FORM, NOR ANY OTHER POISONS
EXCEPT BY PRESCRIPTION.

F. T. OSBORN

Edgartown buzzed, then debated. The *Boston Globe* ran a front-page story. It was picked up by the Associated Press, which circulated the story widely, in a version that had a comic coloration, that made Freeman seem like a Yankee eccentric. When *Life* magazine sent a photo-journalist to do a story, Freeman said no flatly and refused to be persuaded.

In time to come, he was to lose the store, but as long as he owned it, no tobacco was sold there.

One morning, leafing aimlessly through a long-dead whaling captain's journal he had bought at a rummage sale, he came upon a long passage on the subject of ambergris and its uses. He had been working, unsuccessfully, with various forms of chlorophyll to make his preparation non-odoriferous. Could ambergris be the answer? A week later, he acquired a sampling of the stuff and began a new series of experiments. When they proved to be promising but less than ideal, it occurred to him to try combinations. The end of his search came soon after the first of these.

He tested the new substance on himself again and again. He sought out swampland and marshes. He walked through particularly infested parts of State Forest. His substance worked.

He engaged a group of twelve high school students to assist him. Three boys and three girls became a control group; the remaining six used his spray. The results were dramatically affirmative.

Freeman treated his group to a Boston weekend celebration complete with rooms at the Parker House, theatres, jazz concerts, and a shopping spree.

His next step involved legal consultation, a trip to

New York to consult with patent attorneys who specialized in pharmaceutical products.

When, at length, they called to tell him that it was safe to proceed, he went to Cincinnati. There, he met with the head of the firm he most trusted. Acceptance was immediate. A simple letter agreement was drafted and signed; the full documents would take months.

Freeman's new partner/friend took him to the airport. As they parted, the man asked, "Well, sir—how does it feel to be a millionaire?"

"It feels fine," he replied.

Flying back to New York to meet Sheila, he thought it over. The tycoon had exaggerated. It would be some time before large returns would be forthcoming. Still, his continuing royalties would provide all he needed and would do so for years to come. Perhaps, yes, they might eventually add up to—what did it matter? He had, at last, in his fifties, done something useful. Above all, Sheila would take pride. Nothing mattered more.

Again, his creative thoughts began to center on the Japanese house they would build on Squibnocket Pond. His new affluence (precisely what it was, he reflected, a flowing-in) made it possible for him to think in new categories. Why not buy it *all* in Japan? The wood and stone and parchment? Bring Japanese craftsmen over to erect it and gardeners to do the landscaping? Of course. The only way. It would cost—who cares what it would cost?

He looked forward excitedly to discussing it all with Sheila.

The day was marred. She failed to arrive for their planned meeting at the St. Regis. A special delivery letter came instead on the following day. It was typed and bore as a return address:

Cavendish
P. O. Box 1144
Washington, D.C.

This had been their code for some time.
The letter:

Love—We must go home for a few days. Home. What a word! It is not home to me, nor has it ever been. For some reason, still unknown to me, my presence is not only desired, but imperative. Forgive me. How long can you wait there? How did it all go? Are you as thrilled and pleased and proud and delighted as I am? You could not possibly be. Wait, if you can. I shall do better than my best. Meanwhile, be as happy as you deserve to be. Here is my heart.

S.

He read it several times, tore it into small bits, and flushed it down the toilet. It was a practice of long standing and did not seem as crass as it had in their earlier days. There was, of course, nothing in this particular letter to be concerned about in the event that it were to be lost and found, but the habit was now ingrained.

He phoned his daughter, who was at this time, a graduate student at the University of Texas in Austin.

"Jackson?" (This was his name for her, now that she claimed to have outgrown Jackie.)

"Dad! Where are you?"

"New York. In the splendor of the St. Regis. Guess

94

who else is staying at the hotel? On the same floor, in fact."

"Tell me. I'm too busy to guess."

"Your personal fascinators," he said.

"Not—?"

"Absolutely. Laurence Olivier and Vivien Leigh."

"You don't *mean* it!"

"I do."

"I'm coming right over!" she shouted.

"I wish you would, Jackson. I've got a parcel of grand news and no one to share it with."

"What is it?"

"Not the same on the phone. It's that kind of large once-in-a-lifetime stuff that wants eye-to-eye and watch each other's expressions and then go dancing around the room with no music because the news is the music."

"Dad, will you stop it? You've got me all *unglued!*"

"All right. I'll give you this much. Your old Dad's had a marvelous stroke of good fortune. And there's a chance—no—a *good* chance that you'll be—someday—a rich young lady."

"When?" she asked.

"Maybe pretty soon," he said. "And even as of now, I'm prepared to offer you a sample."

"What're you *talking* about, Cap?"

He trembled. She had not used this name since their regatta days, when he was "Captain" and she . . .

"Well, listen, Mate," he said. "I want you to tell me three things you want—not wishes, mind you, *things*. I can't grant wishes, but I *can* come up with things."

"Are you serious, Cap?"

"Try me."

"How about a new car?" she asked.

"What kind?"

"Studebaker Champion."

"What color?"

"Red."

"What else?" he asked.

"Dad!"

"What else?"

"I'd give *anything* for a bigger apartment, because—"

"You don't *have* to give anything. *I'm* doing the giving today."

"Then it's all right if I—?"

"But not a bigger apartment," he said.

"Why not?"

"I want you to buy a house."

"*What?*" she shouted.

"A small house. You're a house girl, Mate. You were born in a house and raised in a house, and you'll always be happier in a house."

She was crying now. "Cap," she said, "you're a very wise man."

"Yes," he said. "And so *few* people *know* it! Buy a house. Don't look for a bargain—you'll find, later on, that there's no such thing, really—look for a house you want to live in. You can always sell it when you're done with it."

"Thank you," she said.

"What else?"

"What?"

"That's only two," he reminded her. "Studebaker, red. House, small."

"Well, we *could* use some money. There's this terrific script—with one of those sure-fire score parts in it—nobody'll put it on—even for a tryout. We believe in it, though."

"Who's *we?*"

"Me and Brad."

"Who's Brad?"

"The boy I'm living with. And I."

"You don't need money," said Freeman. "You need ministry."

"Oh, no. None of that. I'm not ready for marriage. *He* is. Thinks he is. He's at me all the time," she said.

"Of course. He's after your money!"

They laughed together, then she said, "Don't worry about me, Cap. Please."

"Look here," he said. "What time is it out there?"

"Ten-fifteen A.M."

"All right. Your things. I want you to buy them right now. This offer is only good until six P.M."

"Cap. I think you've gone crazy."

"Do you?"

"But in a nice way."

"Oh."

"The car, yes—but not the house—I can't possibly—"

"Sorry, miss," he said. "By six P.M., or it's all off."

He hung up. A few minutes later, the phone rang. He knew it was Jacqueline, trying to re-establish the connection. He sat, smiling at the phone, but did not answer it.

He lingered in New York for three days. He bought tickets for the Old Vic season, hoping that Sheila would

97

turn up in time to go with him. When she did not, he went to the theatre alone, turned in his extra ticket and later observed with interest, each time, the buyer at his side.

The first night, it was an intense, haggard young man who did not remove his coat and sat clutching a pile of magazines throughout the performance of *Henry IV, Part 2*.

The next night provided a sweet-faced, beautifully dressed, elderly lady. Lost in *Uncle Vanya* on the stage, she clutched Freeman's arm (during the shooting scene), slapped his knee (at all jokes), and finally took his hand and held it tenderly (as an autumnal mood descended on the play's ending).

She applauded vociferously at the end and shouted, "Bravo!" to the actors, but said not a word to Freeman before she left.

On the third night, Freeman felt certain that Sheila would appear and waited until the last possible moment before leaving for the theatre. A double bill consisting of *Oedipus Rex* and *The Critic* was to be played. It was the most spectacular of the Old Vic's presentations, offering Olivier in two widely contrasting roles in a single evening. The crowd crushing around the box office in the hope of last-minute cancellations was greater than ever. Freeman had difficulty turning in his extra ticket as individuals begged him for it. He knew, however, that it was against the law to sell it and pressed his way to the box office.

The lights had already gone down and the curtain up, when a small figure slipped into the seat beside him. Freeman turned and in a brief glance saw that it was an exceedingly attractive young woman. She fished in her handbag, found eyeglasses, put them on, and leaned forward. She gave her full attention to the performance of *Oedipus Rex* and did not change her position by so much as an inch for the next hour and twenty minutes.

At the end, the stunned audience sat in dark silence before exploding into its ovation. The quiet was broken by a husky voice at Freeman's side saying, "My . . . *God!*"

Freeman made a move toward the aisle, but could not pass as the girl was still sitting forward, bolt upright. She was holding onto the back of the seat in front of her.

"May I?" he asked.

"What? Oh. Sorry."

She rose and stepped back.

"Aren't you going out?" he asked.

"No." She smiled. "I know you'll think it's stupid, but I can't believe I got this seat and I'm scared someone may get it away from me if I leave it."

"But you've got a stub, surely," Freeman said.

"I'll say," she responded, opened her fist, and showed him a tiny, damp, pink ball of cardboard.

"Well, there you are, then."

"No. Proves nothing. I was in a show once where—by mistake, actually—they sold out the whole house twice. Two people for every seat. What a night. I've never gotten over it. Go ahead. I wish I *weren't* so neurotic. I'm dying for a cigarette after that. Like you."

"I don't smoke," said Freeman.

"*I* do."

Freeman reached the top of the aisle and returned at

once. The girl, her glasses on her head, was reading the program. She looked up.

"Already?"

"I've got an idea," he said. "You go ahead and smoke. I'll guard your seat. With my life." As she hesitated, he added, "I give you my personal guarantee."

She leaped from her seat and ran up the aisle, which was by now clear.

She returned just as the lights were dimming, sat down, and exhaled a final puff of smoke.

"Thanks," she said.

Freeman threw her a wave.

The Sheridan farce that followed was so spirited and provided such a relief from the just-ended tragedy that the audience's response was manic.

Freeman and the girl looked at each other several times, sharing the fun.

The evening ended in a joyous burst of appreciation from the audience and players alike.

The girl continued to look toward the stage, although the curtain had fallen for the last time.

"Well," she said gravely, "I would say that that is the greatest single evening I've ever spent in the theatre."

"It sure was fine," said Freeman.

"No," said the girl. "I want to change that. The greatest single evening I've ever spent."

They moved up the aisle together.

"Are you the one turned the ticket in?" she inquired.

"Yes."

"Then I certainly want to thank you."

"Not at all."

"What happened?" she asked.

"My wife," he answered, "was delayed. Out of town."

"Oh. Well, I'm sorry for her and glad for me."

"Would you care for a dish of ice cream?" asked Freeman.

She laughed. "Certainly not."

"A drink? Some food?"

"Try 'champagne.' That's the only appropriate thing after a super event like the one tonight."

After a pause, Freeman asked, "Would you care for a glass of champagne?"

"Yes," she replied brightly. "Yes, I believe I would. How'd you guess it?"

They walked toward the Plaza in silence.

"Are you troubled about something?" he asked, halfway.

"Yes," she said. "I'm not sure I should be doing this."

"Doing what?"

"Letting myself be picked up by strange men."

"Oh. Do you think I'm strange?" he asked.

"I meant—stranger."

"That's even *worse*," he said.

The banter broke the tension, and they moved into the Oak Room contentedly.

Freeman asked for the wine list and ordered champagne.

She said, "I was only kidding. Honestly."

"I wasn't," he said. When the waiter and the captain had left, he went on. "My name is Freeman Osborn. I'm a pharmacist. I live in Edgartown, Massachusetts.

I'm fifty-six years old and the top of my life was three days ago. The top up to now, that is."

"I'm Diana Boyle," she said. "How do you do?"

They shook hands, across the table.

"Is that all?" he asked.

"I'm an actress," she said.

"Yes. I gathered that."

"How?"

"You said something earlier on about a show you'd been in."

"Did I?"

"Yes," he said.

"I don't remember. Anyway. I am. At least *I* think so. Hardly anybody else does. So far." The champagne arrived and was served. After half a glass, she went on. "Two parts in three years. A small one in a hit and a big one in a flop. In between, modeling, radio, TV, commercials. You've probably seen me." She struck a pose and quoted, " 'It's irregularity, dear, and that's nothing to worry about *these* days, not since blah blah blah blah blah . . .' It took me nine takes to get that right. They kept saying, 'More sincerity!' What else? I come from Rochester, New York. And I'm not going to tell you *my* age—oh, what the hell? Twenty-four. No. Twenty-five. God! And I live at the Three Arts Club on Eighty-fifth Street, and the bottom of my life is right now."

"Why?"

"Listen. I'm quite dizzy all of a sudden. Maybe it's the champagne on top of I haven't eaten all day. Should I go get some air?"

She looked, more than anything, frightened.

"No," he said. "Food." He signaled the captain, who stepped over at once. "What's ready? What can you bring in a minute?"

"A minute?" the captain repeated. "Roast beef, cold chicken aspic?"

"How about a minute steak?" asked Freeman.

"Oh, no," said the captain. "That will take ten, fifteen minutes at least."

Freeman and Diana laughed. The captain could not imagine why.

"All right, then," said Freeman. "Roast beef. Right away, would you? I'd appreciate it. The young lady doesn't feel well."

She sat, resting her head on her fingertips, listening wanly as Freeman talked about the plays they had just seen, about the Old Vic in London during the war, and about the Oak Room where it was men only for lunch.

The food arrived.

"Eat it slowly," he advised.

It worked. She felt better, drank more champagne. He ordered ice cream for them both.

"See?" he said. "A dish of ice cream after all."

"I feel fine, really. Sorry to be such a drag."

"Why *didn't* you eat all day?" he asked. "Forget? I've done that sometimes—working and—"

"No, no," she replied. "It was—well, I had a reading —a *second* reading, actually—I'm up for a part in— anyway—I got in too late for dinner at the club and I didn't want to—well."

"Not economy, for God's sake?"

He noticed that his question had made her blush.

"Was it?"

She nodded, once.

"But that damned ticket tonight. Six dollars!"

"That's right," she said, brazening it out.

"You paid six dollars for a theatre ticket and didn't *eat?*"

"Yes. I mean, no, I didn't."

"You're out of your mind," he said.

She looked at him and said quietly, "No, I'm not, Mr. Osborn."

"Anything more?" he asked.

"No, thank you. I'm fine."

"Check, please," he called. Then to her, "*Now* some air."

As they left the hotel on the Central Park side, he asked, "How long since you took a carriage ride through the park?"

"Never," she said.

"Shall we?"

"Why not?"

In an ancient carriage, they moved slowly through the surprising, verdant park.

Freeman spoke. "The bottom of your life, you said. Why?"

"You don't want to hear about it," she replied. "It's boring. It's boring even to *me*."

"Start," he suggested. "If I mind it, I'll ask you to stop."

She hesitated. "I'm thinking of some advice my mother once gave me. She said, 'Never tell a man your troubles.'"

Freeman laughed. "She was right. Your mother was

104

giving you the right steer there. But, after all, I'm not a man in the sense that *she* meant. So go ahead."

"Well," she began. "It's not very original. Man trouble."

"Could be worse," he said. "*Men* trouble."

"I've had that, too. But right now, it's just one. One stubborn no-good sonofabitch bastard I'm so madly in love with I can *taste* it! Look. Even only this—*talking* about him—and I've got wet palms and my mouth's dry and I don't know if you can hear my heart going, but *I* can."

Taxis and cars sped past, overtaking their carriage and giving them the impression that they were traveling even more slowly than they were. The pace seemed to be helpful, breaking the headlong velocity of the city about them. They rode in silence for a time, each comforted by the presence of the other. At Seventy-second Street, she spoke again.

"Love," she said. "You want to know about love, ask me. This is my fourth time but it's my first time. Does that make sense?"

"Certainly."

"When it's right, it's supposed to have a balance, right? Give and take. Inhale, exhale. Adjust."

"Where is he?" asked Freeman.

"In Maine," she replied miserably. "He's a potter."

"Is that supposed to impress me?"

"What do you mean?"

"I've never heard of them," said Freeman.

"Who? Oh! No. I don't mean he's a *Potter*. His name is Rosen. He's a *potter*. He makes pots and bowls and urns and like that."

"Oh," said Freeman. "I see."

"Actually, he's probably the greatest living potter in the world today."

"Then what's the trouble?"

"This. I'm here and he's there. See, what *I'm* doing—*doing!*—I mean *trying* to do—I have to do here. There's no other place I *can* do it. What *he* does, he could do anywhere. But he won't."

"Why not?"

"He says he's not ready. He isn't on his own yet. He works with that old Scott Cromwell—well, *for* him, really. Room and board and that's it. So how're we *ever* going to put together the seven thousand?"

"What seven thousand?" asked Freeman.

She looked at him as though he were not quite bright and said, "—that he *needs*. To go on his *own*."

"Oh, *that* seven thousand."

"You know. Equipment and a kiln and a wheel. Also a place—and time. He figures a year and half to get to be self-supporting."

"He sounds like a practical chap."

"Of course. That's his trouble. He's *too* practical. So we made this plan. Work and save. Thirty-five hundred each, and as soon as we've got it, he comes down, we set up and even get married, if it's not too expensive." She sighed. "That was over a year ago he figured out the scheme. So guess where we are? He's got forty-five dollars from two pieces he sold and I'm sixteen hundred in debt. And on top of that, it's after one, and I've got to be in by two—that's the rule—after that, the door's locked and you need a letter from the Secretary of Defense to get in."

They abandoned the carriage abruptly. The driver became abusive and continued his harangue until Freeman said, "Keep the change."

He hailed a taxi and told the driver to hurry, please. They reached 85th Street and Broadway by one-thirty.

"A nightcap," said Freeman.

Diana giggled at the old-fashioned locution.

In a booth at the Bretton Hall Hotel bar, she ordered beer, which surprised him.

"You're sure?" he asked.

"It's my usual," she answered.

He asked for J&B on the rocks and said, "Excuse me."

She assumed he was going to the men's room, and considered going to the ladies', but what the hell, why bother? She would be home soon. Might as well save the quarter.

She was halfway through her beer when he returned.

"I hope you don't mind," she said. "All that talking made me thirsty."

"Cheers," he said, and drank.

"You're a nice man," she said. "You know what I was sitting here and thinking while you were away?"

"No."

"About this girl I met in Vienna two years ago, when I went over for the USO. I was general understudy and assistant stage manager for this company of *Oklahoma*. And the three weeks we were there, we all met different people and went out a lot and talked. It was hard, some of it, on account of language, but there was this one girl—what a beauty! and a terrific actress besides—who spoke English perfectly, and I said to her, 'You ought to come to America. You couldn't miss. Either coast. Or both.' And she said, 'Oh, no. That's not for me. Not my life at all.' So I asked her, 'Why not?' And she said, 'Well, let me try to explain. A few weeks ago, in the first week of the May Wine, a young lawyer I know telephoned to me one morning and asked if I was free. I said yes, so he closed his office and picked me up, and we drove out into the country. There we walked and talked and finally went to an inn and bought a picnic basket and two small bottles of wine and went to the woods and ate and drank and talked about—oh, all sorts of things: politics and travel and sex and theatre. Then we lay down and had a nap. When we woke up, we took the basket back to the inn and had a cup of tea and drove back to the city so that he could have an early dinner with his wife and three children, and I had a date with my beau. He dropped me at my flat and he thanked me and I thanked him and he kissed my hand and we parted. Now the question is: "Could this happen to me in New York?"' And I said, 'No, I don't think so.' And she said, 'In Hollywood?' And I had to say, 'No. Definitely not.' So she said, 'Well, that's why I don't want to go to America.'"

"Fascinating," said Freeman.

"I must say," she said, "I thought it all seemed really unreal—what she told me—until tonight. Now it's happened to me, sort of. Listen. I hate to, but I have to go."

He handed her an envelope.

"What's this?" she asked.

"It's a loan," he said. "I consider it a good investment

—one of my best. Now it's up to you and Mr. Rosen not to let me down."

As he spoke, she opened the envelope and looked at the check she found inside it. It was drawn on the Edgartown National Bank and made out to her in the amount of seven thousand dollars.

She gasped and handed it back, saying, "No! My God! What *is* this? I—"

"Take it," he insisted.

"For God's sake," she said, "Jerry'll think—God *knows* what—"

Freeman stood up and looked down at her angrily.

"Look here," he said. "If Jerry believes anything other than what you tell him, you've no business marrying him anyway. Now shut up and let's go, or you'll be locked out."

They walked swiftly through the lobby, down 85th Street to the Three Arts Club.

"Look at me," she said huskily on the way. "I'm staggering. On one beer."

At the door, he took her hand and kissed it gracefully.

"Vienna, my ass!" he said and walked away. He heard her laugh behind him. At the corner, he turned. She waved to him from the doorway and went in.

Freeman walked all the way back to the St. Regis buoyantly.

He never saw Diana Boyle again, nor was he ever to meet Jerry Rosen, but the seven thousand dollars was repaid within two years with carefully calculated interest.

From time to time, he recognized Diana on a television show, and once he saw her on Broadway in a Neil Simon play.

A year or so after the encounter, Freeman received an invitation to a private showing of Jerry Rosen's most recent work at a 57th Street gallery, thought of going, but decided, at the last minute, against it. . . .

XIX

. . . ON THE PORCH of the Falmouth Sunset House, Freeman was again remembering. This time, pain flooded through him, beginning in the pit of his stomach, it seemed, and reaching—octopuslike—in all directions. When it had permeated him completely, it turned into a sickening nausea. What he recalled this time was Sheila's pregnancy and their never-born child.

In all their years, it was the one time he had seen her weep—and she did so bitterly, abandonedly, tragically. Yes, he had thought, as he held her close to him, but providing small comfort. No wonder. She is weeping for both of us, perhaps for all three of us.

Years had made the memory more vivid: its colors richer, its sounds vibrant. He now saw a kind of beauty in that lean contorted face, in the wracked body.

Could they have taken another road? Had there been, at that time, a better way they failed to see? The questions haunted him, but even now, he was unable to think of a course of action other than that which they had followed. . . .

XX

SHE HAD GONE TO NEW YORK, ostensibly to see a specialist. Actually, he was a gynecological surgeon (recommended by her Washington physician) who operated a small, furtive clinic in Gramercy Park.

She was confined there for five days. Thomas phoned her each day, precisely at twelve noon. (She could almost hear the soft, self-effacing voice of Mrs. Roos saying, "It's just coming on to noon, Mr. Van Anda. Shall I get Mrs. Van Anda now?")

Freeman came to New York and visited her at the clinic anywhere from six to eight times each day. He managed to make his calls seem perfectly natural and above suspicion simply by buying a chauffeur's uniform and wearing it. He became, during this time, Mrs. Van Anda's "driver" and brought in newspapers (one at a time), magazines, books, flowers, and toys. He went on errands and spent hours each day at her side. As a final obfuscating touch, he began an outrageous flirtation with her nurse, a pink-faced Scottish redhead called Miss Niven.

Once, when Sheila and Freeman were alone, she asked, "Is that absolutely necessary?"

"Is what, ma'am?"

"Those come-hither eyes you make at Miss Niven. The poor girl's in a tizzy. Did you notice just now?

She put the wrong end of the thermometer in my mouth."

"You're lucky she didn't put it into *my* mouth."

"What I mean is," said Sheila, "I'll be out of here in two or three days—and you'll be leaving damage behind."

"There's a broken heart for every light on Broadway," said Freeman gravely. Miss Niven came in. He stepped away from Sheila, said, "Yes, ma'am," executed a swift, two-fingered salute, and winked at the nurse before he left.

When Sheila left the clinic, she went to the St. Regis for a week. So did Freeman.

Their time together was interrupted only at noon each day by the customary telephone call from Washington.

Freeman took care of Sheila expertly, in the manner of a superlative male nurse.

"Oh, thank you," she said one evening after he had carefully bathed her and given her a gentle massage using almond oil and rose water. "I feel deliciously spoiled."

"Thank *you*," he said.

"You really are a superb nurse," she said, closing her eyes.

"I don't know," he said morosely. "I try my best, but sometimes I think that—well, maybe we ought to get—you know, what's her name—Miss Niven to come over."

She opened her eyes and tried to kick him. He jumped away, his hands covering his crotch. She kicked again and missed.

"Please, ma'am!" he said. "If you don't calm down, we'll have to restrain you."

"How?" she asked.

"Like this," he replied, and lay down beside her, and held her in his arms. In a few minutes, she was asleep. He watched her as she slept, wondering from time to time what was going on inside that beloved head. At times, she smiled gently; often there would be a frown; once, a troubled moan. When this occurred, he moved her head with a caress and broke the dream. Presently, she was smiling again.

He took five careful minutes to slide out of bed so as not to awaken her. He closed her bedroom door silently, called room service, and ordered dinner.

As he served her dessert (Peach Melba), she asked, "How is it we never seem to quarrel, love?"

"Would you like to? I'm game."

"There must be times when you disagree with me. Is it that you don't say so?"

"Of course."

"Like when?"

He thought, served himself, and sat opposite her. "I can't remember," he said. "Shows you how important it was."

"Thomas and I quarrel a good deal. I think he enjoys it."

"Do *you?*"

"Not at all."

"Why do it, then?"

"I have to. I have to express myself or I'll explode. You've no idea how difficult it is—Washington life. We don't—we can't—say what we think and feel in public.

It all needs to be calculated and considered for possible effect. So many things are supposed to be confidential, but hardly any are. We thrive on gossip and inside stuff. I suppose that's why men in government are always taking it out on their wives. Life is so frustrating for most of them. Some of the wives fight back, others simply bear it as a hazard of political life. In either case, it certainly makes for a tense atmosphere."

"We used to quarrel," he mused. "Colette and I. When we were first married. They were violent, some of them. Once she threw a kettle at me. Missed, but scalded herself. Another time, she slapped me. I've often wondered why I didn't slap her back. I'm glad I didn't, though. It would only have led to more of the same and first thing you know, it's a habit. And I can think of *nothing* more boring than two people going through life, cuffing each other around."

"*I* can," she said.

"But that was only in the early years, in the beginning. Later on, we lost interest. Not in each other, you understand, but in our marriage."

"I'm afraid I *don't* understand."

"Well, she's interested in me—she must be—otherwise she wouldn't go on finding so many faults in me and in what I do and how and when. She's interested in me the way a person is in a possession—a house or a horse. And *she* interests *me* as an unnatural phenomenon."

"Unnatural?"

"She doesn't change. Everything in nature changes. Every living thing. Not only nature. Inanimate things, too. Paintings or music. They change, because *we*

change. I'm always hearing new things in old music—
aren't you? And in familiar paintings, seeing things I've
never seen before. Two weeks ago I read—maybe for
the fifth or sixth time—*The Mysterious Stranger* by
Mark Twain. I swear there were scenes in it that
weren't there before. Change. But not Colette. She's
fixed, frozen in amber. She thinks now what she thought
twenty years ago. She hates our town, as you know, but
no more or less than she did when she first encountered
it. If she got to hate it enough, she'd leave it, I suppose.
But no—it's just a—well, a sort of static distaste. And
she lives with it."

They finished dessert.

"I've eaten too much," she said.

"The least you could do, after me over a hot stove
all day."

"That's why."

"All right, now," he said. "Onto the sofa and feet
up."

"No, I like it here."

"Feet up," he said. "Or no coffee."

"There you are!" she said. "We're quarreling."

"At last," he said.

He made her comfortable on the sofa in the sitting
room, and covered her with a blanket. He gave her
coffee and brought his own to have beside her in a
drawn-up easy chair.

When they finished their coffee, they looked at each
other, into each other. They lived together in silence
for an hour, savoring their joy in each other.

She fell asleep. He leaned over, put his forehead on
the arm of the sofa, and in a few minutes joined her in
happy oblivion.

XXI

SHEILA AND FREEMAN met for a midweek weekend at the Ritz in Boston.

As he came through the door of her suite, he knew that something was wrong. He did not ask what, nor did she tell him, until some time after they had lovingly commingled.

At dusk, lights came on in the Public Gardens and on the Boston Common. Neon began to slice the sky, and the Charles River took on a new aspect.

They did not put lights on in the suite, but sat or moved about in the restful dimness.

He knew that bad news was coming and wanted to stave it off as long as possible. He explained, in minute detail, all that had happened in Cincinnati. She thrilled to it. He told her of his talk with Jacqueline and of his encounter with Diana Boyle.

"You're a fairy tale!" said Sheila.

"Are you hungry?" he asked.

"Not yet."

"All right, then," he said. "Tell me the worst."

She waited, collected her thoughts, and began.

"Thomas is going to run for the Senate."

"I'll be damned!"

"He resisted it until they proved to him that there's no chance of his losing."

"What does it mean to us?"

"Another year or so," she said. "He put it to me plainly, said it was up to me. If I didn't want to wait, he'd understand, and so on. But if we divorced now, he wouldn't run; couldn't, in fact."

"So it goes," he said. "Shall we have dinner here or go to Charles's?"

"Here, please."

They talked of many things in the course of the next two days. They slept little and at odd times. They discussed the differences in their life that might come about as a result of Freeman's deal. They considered the possibility of going abroad to live for a time, but always their thoughts and their plans returned to the Island and, more particularly, to Squibnocket Pond.

"That's where we began, really, and that's where we should end," she said.

"We're never going to end," he said. "We're going to live forever. The man who invented the insect repellent will now perfect a death repellent."

"Congratulations," she said.

Talk of a trip to Japan occupied them for one whole afternoon.

He got out a new Japanese phrase book he had found at the Old Corner Bookstore, looked up "I love you," and said, "Anata wah ah-ee shee mas!"

"Thank you," she said. "What a curious phrase to put in a phrase book!"

"You never know when you'll need it," said Freeman.

"I need it right now," she said.

At dinner that evening Sheila became aware of Freeman's preoccupation. They had grown to be unfailingly sensitive to each other's moods.

"What is it, love?" she asked.

He shook his head briefly.

"Come on," she urged.

"Jacqueline," he said. "Trouble."

"Oh, dear. What?"

"I try not to burden you with problems——"

"I wish you would," she said.

"I think I mean with *her* problems. Anyway. While she was at Radcliffe, she met this Harvard fellow—a drama major—and went off to Texas with him. I didn't mind *that*—that she went—if that was what she wanted. It was the *why* she went that bothered me. It was just to get away from us—from her home and the damned abrasive atmosphere. So I felt responsible. Well. Anyway. A few months ago—in April, they were married."

"I remember."

"And now it's over."

"Already? Why?"

"Delicate to explain. A polite way, I guess, is to say because of her husband's—uh—sexual ambivalence."

"Oh, Lord."

"So now she's embittered. Hates men, distrusts marriage, more inhibited than ever, and is escaping into science. She's gone to work for UNESCO. Leaves for Africa in a week. I'm sick about it."

"My love," said Sheila, "haven't you learned that we can't live other people's lives for them? She has to be allowed to make her own mistakes. And who knows? Maybe it'll turn out to be not a mistake at all." . . .

XXII

. . . How RIGHT SHEILA HAD BEEN! As always, instinctively wise and knowing and gentle.

From Africa, Jacqueline had been assigned to a month-long convention in Venice. There she met Dr. Max Tarloff, an American scientist concerned with the world's food supply. Venice did its work, and after a swift and explosive love affair, she and Max were married.

Freeman recalled her detailed account of how, when the convention ended, they bought a car and toured Italy, with special emphasis on Tuscany: Florence, Siena, Collodi, Pisa, and two days on the superb beach at Alassio.

They lay side by side, hand in hand, drenched in Italian oil.

"Next to one I know in America," said Max, "this must be the best beach anywhere."

"Terrific," said Jacqueline, sleepy in the sun. She sighed happily. "Super. And what beach is that? In America."

"South Beach," he said. "On Martha's Vineyard."

Jacqueline's body gave a short, convulsive twitch. She lay motionless for a time, then said, "Ha, ha."

"What?"

"Some joke."

He turned toward her and lay on his side. "What?"

"I'm *not* falling for it."

"For what?"

"That tease," she said. "You've found out that's where I'm from so you give me that guff. South Beach, indeed."

"What're you talking about?" he asked. "*Nobody's* from South Beach."

"The Vineyard," she said. "That's where I'm from."

"You are?"

She turned to him, propped herself up on an elbow, saw that he was in earnest and said, "Yes. Of course. Edgartown."

"Well, I'll be damned."

"Why?"

"How come I never found you?" he asked. "I've spent every summer there for fifteen years—except three war ones. And four year-round ones."

"No! Where?"

"Chilmark."

"Oh, no wonder," she said, lying down again. "We don't speak to Chilmark."

"Why the hell not?"

"Too intellectual."

"I own a house in Chilmark," he said. "Well, not a house, really. More of an intellectual shack."

"Let's go there."

"All right."

"How'd you *get* to the Island, anyway?" she asked. "Looking for me?"

"No," he said. "I was with the Marine Biological Institute at Woods Hole—couldn't find a place I liked to live—so, finally, the Island—and I commuted. On the ferry."

"I've crossed on that ferry a thousand times. Probably with you, several."

"Amazing, isn't it? There we are—the two of us—and we don't meet until here."

"We did a little more than meet, my boy. Or has it slipped your mind?"

"What? That we're engaged? Of course not."

"You don't frighten me," she said. "Married. And I've got the papers to prove it."

"They're in Italian. Maybe they're a fishing license."

"My Italian," she said, "is *bellissimo*."

"It goes to show," he said. "There must be a guiding intelligence."

"Yuh. I hope he's more intelligent than he was last time."

"What was *that?*"

"Say, you hardly know *anything* about me, do you?" she asked.

"I know enough."

"You didn't know I was from the Vineyard, and you don't know I was married to a faggot—"

Max was instantly interested.

"A *real* faggot?"

"Devout," she said.

"You must tell me about it."

"Maybe," she said. "Some day. When I know you better."

Freeman smiled as he recalled this excited account by Jacqueline. . . .

XXIII

The year of Thomas Van Anda's campaign was a difficult one for Freeman and Sheila. She had not realized the extent to which it was necessary that she be involved. Still, what began as a burdensome duty soon developed into an exciting challenge. Not only victory, but decisive victory became the aim. The closer they moved toward the day of election, the more time she and her husband spent in Indiana, and for the last four months, they remained there.

In Denver, Jacqueline awaited the birth of her first child. As the scheduled time approached, Freeman flew to join her. Halfway there, he began to berate himself. It seemed, all at once, a foolish move, perhaps intrusive. He thought of returning immediately upon arrival, but the minute he saw Max, he knew that he was needed.

Max, the cool and disciplined man of science, had gone to pieces.

"I've seen nervous fathers," Freeman told him. "I believe I was one myself, but you take the cake."

"Sorry. A million things can happen. I wish I were ignorant. I've got too much physiology in my head, that's one of the troubles."

Freeman sat with him, walked, drank, stayed awake —and on the morning of the birth, actually held his trembling hand.

At the nurse's smiling nod, Max collapsed and was given sedation.

Freeman's grandson, eventually named Seth (a continuing family name), held him, hypnotically, for a month.

He was fascinated by the tiny creature struggling to become a human being. He reflected for hours on the mysterious flotsam-jetsam circumstance of existence, on the gossamer thread of life that had culminated in the tiny creature writhing and wriggling in the bassinet. Colette and her Gallic forebears; his own ancestors crossing the Atlantic somehow, breaking with the Puritans, moving to the Island. There, conquering land and sea and seasons. Fishing, then whaling, and, finally, fishing again. Max's parents, meeting in steerage. His father, from Poland. His mother, from Lithuania. Both en route to the promise of freedom, and gold in the streets. New York. Marriage. His father beginning as a peddler, ending as a successful leather-goods merchant. His mother, working in a shirtwaist factory until the day before his birth.

Now this lad. So much of the world in him. He would need it all—and more—in the unknowable years to come.

On his way east, Freeman stopped in Indianapolis.

From his hotel—motel, actually, he realized—he phoned.

"Mrs. Van Anda, please."

"May I ask who's calling?" a man's impatient voice inquired.

"Yes, of course. Mr. Cavendish. I'm a personal friend."

"Hold on."

A babble of voices. Typewriters clacking.

Freeman visualized the "smoke-filled room" so typical of the American political scene.

"John?"

Her voice, speaking the rest of his fictitious name, startled him.

"Yes," he said. "John."

"What on earth brings you to Indianapolis?" she asked, acting.

"Love," he said.

"How nice," she said. "And can you stay long enough to see him?"

"Well, yes. If forever's long enough."

"We'll try, of course," she said. "But you can imagine what a time this is for us. We live like planes on a schedule."

"Even planes have to come down once in a while."

"Where are you?"

"The Mohawk Motor Inn," he said, urging her.

"I see."

"I could pick you up," he said. "I've rented a car. Will. And drive you right to my door. It's very private. I'm sure you want privacy these days."

"Yes. Still, it's difficult."

"I don't care," he said.

She continued in a voice so low that he had difficulty hearing her. "No one knows us anywhere—but here and now—we're sort of celebrities. If we weren't, a million dollars or so would've been wasted."

"But listen," he said, "I'm sure if you—"

He stopped as the telephone made a clicking noise, followed by a series of soft rat-a-tats.

"Hello?" he said.

"Oh. Sorry," said a woman's voice. "Thought the line was free. Will you be long? Who's on?"

"Me, Mamie," said Sheila. "Mrs. Van Anda."

"Oh, I'm *sorry!*"

Click.

"Tricky," said Sheila. "As you see."

"I'll wait here," he said. "I won't move."

Thirty hours later, she called him. He had not left his room.

"It looks impossible," she said.

"I'll wait."

"I mean hopeless."

"Nothing's hopeless."

"Thank you, love," she said.

That night, he attended a rally at the Speedway.

He saw her on the brightly lighted platform, looking more radiant than ever before. He moved closer, then closer still.

At one point, photographs were being made. Endless handshaking with approved supporters.

At length, the Van Andas alone.

"Kiss 'er, Senator," shouted a photographer.

"Go ahead!"

"Now!"

"Wait!"

"Hold it!"

"Go!"

Thomas Van Anda obliged, after which his press representatives moved in and dispersed the cameramen.

The speeches were about to begin.

Freeman had made his way to a seat in the fourth row on the side. He kept his eyes on Sheila. In time, she saw him, looked away, looked back, smiled, looked in the other direction, waved and blew a kiss. Then she looked at him again as the first of the speeches began. Her face remained in repose, as did his. The din faded for them and in the silence, across the space between them, they exchanged multitudes.

Freeman waited another day, then left Indianapolis. He felt curiously satisfied. He had seen his love.

Thomas Van Anda won the election easily. He took his wife to Nassau for a month's holiday, and returned to Washington.

Sheila was occupied for two months in finding a Georgetown house, furnishing it, and staffing it.

A summer arrangement was worked out, and she phoned Freeman to tell him the happy news.

"We're taking the Bliss house on North Water Street for six months," she said. "May through October. I'm going to headquarter there and Thomas is going to come up for weekends—when he can. In the recess he'll have to go home, of course. But I'll stay in Edgartown. This has been a too-tiring time. The campaign and then getting settled in. I'm exhausted. I need a rest."

"You've earned it, my love," he said.

"I think—no—I *know* our life is beginning, my darling."

Freeman flew to France to confer with Colette.

After a few soggy amenities, he said, "What I propose is this: you're to receive half my royalties in perpetuity. Whatever you get will belong to you or to anyone you choose to give it to or leave it to. I'm told that this half share may be worth as much as a hundred thousand a year for ten or twenty or more years."

"So," she said. "We have become wealthy."

"Yes," he said. "I have."

"And what you wish now is to buy me off, yes?"

"I wouldn't have put it so crudely, but—"

"Oh, yes. I am crude."

"I'm not asking for much, Colette. Only for an end to something that doesn't really exist."

"You wish to marry again? With someone else?"

(Her extended stays in France had begun to interfere with her English.)

"Possibly," he said.

"Then my answer is no. Not for money. I am no whorelady."

"I honestly don't see the connection."

"And in *each* case, as we are man and wife, the half is to me no matter. I have spoken to many advocates— here and in Boston."

"Very well," he said and handed her a document. "Show this to your advocates and then tell me what you want to do."

He left abruptly.

Her lawyer confessed that he did not fully comprehend the document, since he was not sufficiently familiar with the intricacies of American tax-exempt charitable foundations. However, there was a large American firm with offices in Paris. He would consult someone there.

Having done so, he explained that the paper Freeman

had given her outlined the setting up of an irrevocable trust fund into which Freeman's share of the royalties would flow, after which they would be funneled by its trustees (the Edgartown National Bank) to such pharmaceutical research as they deemed worthy.

She insisted upon meeting with the American lawyer, who explained the matter to her, this time in English.

"But he can do this? He has the rights?"

"Yes."

"But half is mine, no?" she asked.

"No."

"Why not?"

The lawyer shrugged.

Colette went on. "He gives away of my money and your country says yes?"

"Well, it's not actually yours until you've got it. And, of course, he's giving *his* away, too."

"No," she said bitterly. "No, he is *not!* No."

Her next meeting with Freeman, their last, was charged with passion.

"You would do this, eh?" she shouted. "You would give away the millions only to spite me?"

"No, Colette. Just to save us—both of us—from drowning in bitterness."

Their meeting dragged on, their argument traveled its circular route, nothing was resolved.

Freeman returned to the Island. A month later, through a formal communication from her lawyers to his, he learned that Colette was prepared to divorce him pursuant to the conditions they had discussed.

He called Sheila and together they jubilantly planned a celebration. Thomas made no objection to the suggestion that she wanted to take a trip through New England to see the wildflowers. In fact, he encouraged it.

In a rented Airstream trailer, Sheila and Freeman made their way north. The convenience of not having to trouble about hotel or motel arrangements overwhelmed them.

"You're part of a lovely lie of mine," he said one evening as they cooked together. They were attempting a bouillabaisse, having collected the ingredients from roadside stands all day.

"How nice!" she said.

"Yes. I redid my will last Thursday."

"Shut up."

"No," he said. "Lawyers tell us sometimes that a will should be examined at least once a year."

"See your dentist twice a year," she intoned, "rewrite your will once a year. . . . I don't think I *have* a will."

"Where there's a way, there's a will," he said, with a comic leer.

"What? You mean—oh." She got it and laughed.

"Should anything happen to me," he said, "say as a result of eating this scary-looking bouillabaisse—my half of the proceeds of the windfall goes to you."

"Windfall, my eye," she said. "A great, brilliant, valuable *discovery!*"

"Thank you."

"And I hope you're joking," she said.

"Of course not. I want you to have it. You deserve it a hell of a lot more than she deserves *her* half."

"You're mad—sweetly mad—but mad."

129

"Why?"

"It must never happen—but say it did—if it did—how could I ever explain the—"

"Please!" he interrupted. "You must give me credit for a few brains—say one or two? Don't you think I've thought all that out?"

"Have you?"

"Certainly. And the codicil—if I do say so myself—is a dilly."

"Go on."

"'To my friend Sheila Hanrahan Van Anda,'" he said as if reading, "'I bequeath the interest in the proceeds of All-Off now owned by me. All agreements between myself and the Sebring Corporation shall be transferred to her, her heirs or assignees in perpetuity and without restriction of any kind.'"

"It's not a dilly so far," said Sheila.

"Wait," he continued. "'A word of explanation as to the reason for this bequest may be seemly, in view of the fact that Mrs. Van Anda and I have enjoyed no more than a casual acquaintanceship.'"

"That will is null and void right there," she said.

"Oh, no. 'However, Mrs. Van Anda, in a visit to my store one day in May 1927, asked me if such a product existed. When I replied in the negative, she suggested that it would be well if it did. On subsequent occasions, she urged me to attempt the development of such a product and became, as it were, an associate. It is to her that I owe not only the end of my search but the beginning.'"

"Yes," she said. "That *is* a dilly. Or do I mean whopper?"

130

"Thank you."

"No, my darling. Thank *you*. And now please see to it that it never comes to me."

"I'll do my best," he said. "I hope this thyme is going to work."

"Better if it were fresh," she said.

"Yes."

They returned to the Island and spent the three final days of their adventure on Squibnocket Pond.

Before they parted, she told him that she was leaving, with her husband, for Spain, Italy, Greece, and Yugoslavia to be gone for five weeks; an important senatorial junket. There was no way out, but this would be the last of the trips. A promise.

Freeman was jolted.

"I *couldn't* tell you before," she said. "It would have spoiled our time."

"I'm so impatient, my love," he said. "Oh, well."

When she had gone, he spent sleepless or troubled nights for two weeks. Then, on an impulse, he took a sleeping bag and went out to the pond. It was better there.

The following morning, his first customer was Ollie. He smiled. Ollie and his antics, his gossip, and his fibs rarely failed to amuse Freeman.

"Mornin', Doc."

"Ollie."

"I need me a bottle of that there Geritol."

"O.K. Something you did or something you're going to do?"

"Both. I been up half the goddam night helpin' Rosella close up the Bliss house for them Van Andas."

131

"What?" Freeman waited for the joke. Houses were never closed in July. Never.

"Yup. The big man hisself—the senator—come up to do the supervising. With his secretary—not a bad piece, by the way. Damn! If there's one thing I hate more'n a senator, it's a *supervisor*."

Freeman, in a panic, heard himself shout, "What the hell are you talking about, Ollie? You and your bloody jokes can be a real pain in the ass sometimes, you know it?"

"Hey, there!" said Ollie, holding up an admonishing finger. "Hey, now there! What's hit *you?* You got no call to chew me out, mister. I can take my trade elsewhere."

"I'm sorry, Ollie. Just tell me what you know, please."

"Not much. He flew in yesterday to close up, that's all, seein' as how his old lady just *cooled*."

A sound escaped Freeman. Ollie took it to be a question.

"I thought you'd heard. Yup. Joined the majority, she did, as they say. In Europe someplace. Or Greece. Hell of a time gettin' her back in the country, they say. The remains, that is. Probably couldn't have done it at all if he hadn't've been a senator."

He went on talking. Freeman was watching his lips but now, oddly, no sound emanated.

Freeman began to suspect that this was a dream. No, a nightmare. The color left the store. He saw it all and Ollie in fuzzy black and white.

Now Ollie was touching him.

"You all right, Doc? Say, listen, long as I'm here,

slip me three rubbers, will y'? I may be gettin' my ashes hauled tonight over in Oak Bluffs."

Freeman went through the motions of a transaction. Ollie started out. The bell rang, startling Freeman. He saw Ollie leave. He was alone. He began to cry, the sobs originating in the pit of his stomach. He tried to move into the back room, but stumbled. He held onto doors and counters, trying to regain equilibrium. His knees gave way and he sank to the floor. There he remained, kneeling. He wanted to stop. What if someone were to come in? His brain sent signals that went unobeyed. Now he was two beings: the first, physically out of control, retching, strangling on held-back tears; the second, a dismayed observer. When, the latter wondered, had he last wept? He tried to remember. Once, when he was sixteen—too old for corporal punishment —his father had insisted on strapping him. What was the offense? Oh, yes. He had taken the horse and buggy without permission. What was more, he had wrecked the buggy. On that occasion, he recalled, it was not so much the physical pain—his father was inexpert—but the spiritual humiliation of removing his pants in the barn and leaning over a wheel of the wrecked buggy while his father, without a word, whipped him ineffectually. He had fought for control, lost, and cried for an hour. Was that the last time? No. Another. It came back to him, surfacing out of long-forgotten days. College. The track team. The 880-yard relay. Running third on the team of four, taking the baton in the new method their coach had developed: a running start, right hand back, palm up, to receive the stick at full speed. But this time: the pass, the passer's spiked toe in his heel; sprawling, sliding in the cinders; the pile-up;

133

blackness. Later, in the locker room, the coach, showing off, had tried to set the break. Freeman had screamed and taken refuge in tears, but—. Had there been any others? None he could think of now. Those two.

His observer self became aware of the fact that the sobs had come to an end. Now what? He stood up and made his way to the back room, to the office. He drank water until it made him nauseous. He started to prepare coffee, but the sight of the two cups on the shelf jarred him and he stopped.

He wondered, for a hope-filled minute, if it were not, possibly, all a mistake. That God-damned drunken Ollie. He might easily have got it all wrong. All wrong. "—old lady." Could that have meant "mother"? Was there someone to call? No. No one. Wait. Henry Hough at the *Gazette* would know.

"Henry? Freeman here. Say, I wanted to ask you about my ad."

"You bet."

"I've been thinking. Maybe I ought to run it on the front page, after all."

"It's up to you, ol' fella."

"What I mean to say is—"

"You got a cold?"

"No, why?"

"Sound like you've got a cold."

"No, must be this damned toy telephone they landed me with."

"About the ad?" asked Henry.

"Oh, yes. See, I don't want to spend any more than I'm spending. Business is—well, could be better. But I wondered what you'd think of using less space, but front page."

Henry laughed. "If I knew the answer to *that*, Freeman, I'd be running the *New York Times*. Running it, hell—I'd *own* it. No. Nobody knows. It's six of one—. Go on your hunch. It's about all you *can* do."

"All right. Let's try it."

"Fine."

"Could I see a proof of the new setup?" asked Freeman.

"Sure. Come on over any time after tomorrow."

"All right."

"Or I could come by your place."

"Either way."

"Come over here, then," said Henry. "Something I'd like to show you, anyway."

His voice took on the sound of finality. Freeman tensed.

"What's new?" he asked, as casually as he could, but heard his voice break. He turned it into a fake cough and added, "Damn! I may be coming down with a cold at that."

"Don't take any medicine, *whatever* you do," said Henry, laughing.

"Anything doing on the Island?" asked Freeman.

"No, not much. Quiet. . . . Oh, I suppose you've heard about poor Senator Van Anda. . . ."

Freeman was on his feet. He *knew* it! That Goddamned drunken Ollie had got it twisted. The *senator*.

"No," he managed quietly. "What *about* him?"

"Lost his wife," said Henry.

After an eternity, Freeman heard, "Hello? . . . Freeman? . . . hello!"

"What?" asked Freeman. "Cut off, I think. This damned phone."

135

"Oh. I was telling you about Mrs. Van Anda dying."

"Yes, I heard you." A deep breath. "What happened?"

"Well, I don't have all the details myself yet. I'm going over there in a bit. Mrs. Roos, you know, his secretary's giving me a copy of the announcement. We want to run something special, of course. After all, a senator's wife. It was a heart attack, I understand. On a boat going to Crete. At least, that's what I've heard. Not official."

"Shame," said Freeman.

"Say, listen. I wouldn't want you to misunderstand me—something I said a moment ago. About us playing it up because—you know, senator's wife. That had a snob sound, and it's not what I meant. She was an awfully nice woman. *Awfully* nice. You knew her, didn't you?"

"Oh, yes. Awfully nice. Did you say Crete? Or Greece?" asked Freeman.

"Crete. But it's all about the same, isn't it?"

Henry glanced up over his roll-top desk. There, framed, as it had been for more than twenty years, was the needlepoint sampler his Betty had given him one Christmas. It read:

2. SILENCE—Speak not but what may
benefit others or yourself; avoid
trifling conversation.

Benj. Franklin
Autobiography
1771–1777

136

"Well, then," said Henry. "We'll shift you to page one and see how you like it."

From the sound, Freeman understood that Henry was anxious to leave off and get on with his day.

"Thanks, Henry. See y'."

"Bye."

It was over then. There was no mistake. What was he to do now? Not in the days to come or weeks or months, but now. Today. This minute. What was the next step? Behave well, correctly. That was what he wanted, above all, to do. A telegram? Sent where? A letter? Flowers. The funeral or services or whatever . . . where and when? How? Does one simply go or do you wait to be asked? What if it is to be in Washington? Could he go then? No, of course not. How would it look? If here, all right. Would it be, could it be? Hadn't she once said—? Did she mean it? We say all sorts of things out of the depth of feeling or from the height of passion. Hadn't *he* once said—he remembered it chillingly—that he would follow her without delay in death? Romantic talk. The very definition of sentimental. Copping out? he asked himself. Not at all. But that is for later. What of now? The immediate *now*?

The immediate now became a month as time, for Freeman Osborn, stood still. He had never before lived in limbo. He understood now what Jacqueline had meant when, after being forced at the age of thirteen to spend the summer of 1938 with her grandparents in Hyères, she had said, "I felt like a zombie the whole time—'un revenant,' *they* say. It's like a whole piece got chopped out of my life."

137

In the years to come, he would spend hours on end trying to recall that lost month—or was it two?

He could recollect pieces, flashes—but only in disorder.

He remembered her laughter. No one in his experience had ever laughed as truly, as fully, or as unpredictably. Four times—or was it five?—the laughter had approached out-of-control hysteria.

Once, during a Christmas pantomime in London. *Peter Pan*. The girl playing the title role had been giving a sickly sweet performance.

"How do you like her?" Sheila asked in the bar in the interval.

"She needs more balls," said Freeman.

Sheila had laughed at that—not hard, but nicely. A few minutes later, however, it happened. The rigging for the flying routine fouled and Peter was left dangling. He was jerked up, then dropped—whereupon he/she began to shout; first, instructions, then imprecations, and finally a burst of Cockney obscenity such as had never been heard in any theatre at any time. Small children were being rushed out, carried out, to escape the language—but against their will because they all wanted to see Peter crash.

Sheila had to be almost carried out herself.

That was one of the times.

Of the others, one was a joke of his. Winter. A fire in the grate. A new Japanese guidebook had been published. He had sent for it, given it to her. He thought, watching her devour its contents, that she resembled a little girl reading *Alice in Wonderland* for the first time.

138

"Last year in Japan was the Year of the Ape," she said. "Guess what it is *this* year?"

"I give up."

"The Year of the Cock," she said.

He leaped to his feet and shouted, "We must go there *at once!*"

How she had laughed.

His office at the back of the store. Shaving. Mrs. Tremaine.

"Are you all right?" she asks.

"Why, yes, of course. Why?"

"Well, just you haven't been home in four days. I got to worrying."

"I've been working, you see. On my project."

"You mean you haven't been out at all?"

"No. I don't think so."

"But what about food?"

"Ice cream," he says.

"Is that *all?*"

"Candy bars. Nuts. Wafers. Cones, did I mention cones?"

"Mr. Osborn, it's not my place to say it. But I like you and always have. You've been a good friend and always kind and helpful in the store. And you ought to stop *drinking!*"

When she had gone, he laughed. What made it all so comical was the fact that he had not, in all this time, had so much as a drop of alcohol. It was there, and he would have had some had he thought of it, but it never crossed his mind.

In any event, he went home that night. He was

grateful to Mrs. Tremaine for having called his absence to his attention.

He is shaking hands with Senator Van Anda. Where? And was this before Mrs. Tremaine or after? Must have been after because she had told him he had not left the store in four days. But perhaps that was not true. It *must* have been before. The senator would not have hung about for four days.

Shaking hands. Mrs. Roos, then the senator. He is one of many in the room. North Water Street.

"—liked you very much, Osborn. *Very* much. Thank you for coming. Most kind. Oh! And London. Do you recall? You were most helpful to her there. To us both, actually. She often said—."

The funeral. Washington. How did he get to Washington? The *Gazette* had, indeed, run a comprehensive obituary. He could bear it now, since it was real. What he could not handle was the story of her life. It was wrong, all *wrong!* It left out the most important part, by far. Somewhere toward the middle . . .

. . . Mrs. Van Anda, wife of Senator Thomas Van Anda of Indiana, had been, with her husband, a summer resident of the Island for sixteen years, usually renting the Tilton house on Summer Street, Edgartown, and latterly the Bliss house on North Water Street. According to information supplied by the senator's office, Sheila Hanrahan was born on her father's cattle ranch near Laramie, Wyoming, on March 3, 1897. Her early education was gained by tutoring. Subsequently, she attended private schools in Denver,

Colorado, and Wellesley College in
Massachusetts. Her major interest
throughout her life was conservation.
To this end, she developed two ancil-
lary skills: photography and linguis-
tics. The former to record, pictorially,
conditions she believed it imperative
to expose; the latter, because she long
believed conservation to be an inter-
national, rather than a national concern. Her work led her to Washington, D.C., where she served in various
capacities: during World War I, with
the Manpower Commission, later in the
Departments of Agriculture and Interior. On November 10, 1922, she married Thomas Van Anda, then attaché
at large in the United States Foreign
Service; stationed variously in Mar-
seilles, France; Kyoto, Japan; Copen-
hagen, Denmark; and Caracas, Venezuela. Later, Assistant Under Secretary
of State; Inspector General to the
ambassadorial branch of the State Department; appointed Chairman of the
Consular Re-organization Commission.
In 1954, he ran successfully for the
Senate, a position he holds at the present time. In addition to her husband,
Mrs. Van Anda leaves one brother,
Cody Hanrahan of Laramie, Wyoming; and a sister, Contessa di Fregosi
of Florence, Italy. Funeral services will
be held at St. Thomas's Church, Washington, D.C., at 10 A.M. on Friday. On
behalf of her many Island friends, the
Vineyard Gazette offers sincere con-
dolences to her bereaved family.

Driving to Boston. Rain. One bad skid, during which he smiled happily, hoping for the worst, the best. Logan Airport. A huge plane. To where? Washington, D.C. The plane goes up and comes down. Trouble? No, it has arrived. A seemingly endless taxi ride to— where was it? He had forgotten to make a hotel reservation and so—with the taxi driver's surly assistance— drove from one to another. Rain. Finally, at the Hay-Adams, he is told that the only space available for the night is a large suite. He takes it, is shown up. Alone, he walks about from room to room. There are four. He reads every piece of literature and *This Week in Washington* and the *Washington Evening Star* right through, not skipping a column. What's this? An innovation. A locked, grilled cabinet contains miniatures of every sort of alcoholic drink. Soda. Tonic. Bloody Mary mix. Locked. A card explains. Key is on the room key. Help yourself and write out a check. *What* a good idea! Not as good as an insect repellent that *works*—but good. The cabinet is opened and provides a blessed numbing. Instructions to the operator to ring at 8:00 A.M., at 8:15 A.M., at 8:30 A.M. To send up breakfast: Double tomato juice, Worcestershire sauce, scrambled eggs, and sausages well-done and dry, rye toast, and double coffee with hot milk. A Mayflower car at 9:15 A.M. A call to the bell captain. A sweaty bellhop appears, is asked to come personally and knock on the door and bring a morning paper, and is given a ten-dollar bill. He smiles and pats Freeman's shoulder. "Will do, ol' timer!" There is no morning in his memory, but the church is there indelibly, in all its musty splendor. There are few mourners. Most of those asked—officially—have sent

142

surrogates. Freeman haunts the shadows at the rear, is regarded suspiciously by an usher, takes a seat in the last pew. The usher approaches and motions him to the front.

"I have a bad throat," Freeman explains hoarsely. "May start coughing. And have to leave."

The usher nods understandingly. Freeman's eyes are on the flower-blanketed coffin.

He has come to grips with the fact of Sheila's death, yet in his mind, she has never been more alive.

They are swimming together, they are in the shower bath at the St. Regis together. She is in tears in the car at Heathrow Airport in England. They are visiting the Frick Collection in New York. They stand before painting after painting, shoulder to shoulder, their bodies in communication. Rain. Where? A taxi. They jump in and find that the back seat overlooks a deep puddle. They sit, feet up, and laugh. Music. They hold hands and listen in the Salle Pleyel. They are at the U. N. Building, in the basement, looking for Kokeshi dolls. Another time. Earlier? Later? A violent unceasing rainstorm. They read aloud a children's book, alternating chapters. What book? What does it matter? A man of consecutive mind, he refuses to go on until he remembers. Cannot. Try. At last. *Stuart Little* by E. B. White. Her laughter. Their discussion of Adlai Stevenson's campaign strategy becomes a bitter quarrel, their first and only. They make up. And they are in one Japanese restaurant after another.

He listens to the music and the prayers and the ceremony and the few words from her friend Dean Acheson—but hears none of it. He is thinking only of what lies inside that coffin. What, he wonders, have they dressed her in? Does it matter? He reconstructs her, anatomically, in his mind, piece by piece. He is gripping the back of the pew before him. He is drenched in perspiration. . . . He is on the ferry, making the long-familiar mini-voyage from Woods Hole to Vineyard Haven. It is night. A sliver of the new moon. Wait, memory. Where is the in-between? Did he join the single file that passed beside the bier? Cannot remember. Try. No use. Did he check out of the Hay-Adams? Did he pay his bill? The flight home? Gone. The ferry, however, is there and clear. The ride home, as well, is fixed in recall, since it marks the first time in his life he ever ran out of gas. He stands at the roadside near Bend in the Road imitating the hitchhikers he has seen so often. Two girls. Too young to be driving. They are great. They take him to the Depot Service Station, wait for him, take him back to his car, help him to start it.

He is home, moving through the days and nights in reflex motion. He suddenly finds himself doing something. Or nothing. Faces. Some of them familiar. He hears himself laugh at a joke. Ollie.

There is a fire one night. He answers the signal, rushes to his volunteer post. It is a difficult fire. All night.

He finds himself fishing. It is the time of the Bass and Bluefish Derby. He wins something.

He sits in his office for one long night and contemplates methods of achieving an end to it all. It will be, simply, part of their life together. A promise. How? It is no more than a question of choice. He is surrounded, literally, by enough substances to put an end to a *thousand* lives. What is to be gained? Peace. An end to those awakenings, feeling fine, stretching—the stretch often so abruptly broken that pain results—and being overwhelmed by the realization of things as they are. What is to be lost? Air, sensation, the morning and the evening. True, but largely meaningless now that it is all unshared.

And what of their Japanese house on Squibnocket Pond? It would never be, now.

That was the night he decided to build it. Why? As a monument, a memorial? Perhaps. Not to her alone, but to them both. Or was he simply postponing, out of cowardice, his own end? His head was throbbing. He swallowed two Empirin codeines, went home, and to bed.

He recognized his condition, knew that he was living in a state of shock, and held on, determined to wait until he had regained his equilibrium before deciding definitely on *anything*.

What began to concern him was the fact that his periods of lucidity and full consciousness were diminishing. He had thought it would be the other way about.

Then came the bad day. Martin Stein, his assistant, had gone off on holiday. Freeman was tending the store.

He was at his worktable, mixing a simple prescription, when he heard the bell.

"Be right with you," he called out. He finished the mixture, put aside the mortar and pestle, washed his hands, dried them, and made his way into the store.

A tall, bronzed, handsome blonde—of the new breed —stood there in a bikini, one hand over her left eye.

"Excuse me," she said. "I know you're not supposed to—my father's a doctor—but I've got something *fierce* in my eye and—"

"*Please!*" he said, staring at her. "*Please!*"

"What?" she said, confused. "Please *what?*" Her hand came away from her eye and he saw that it was, indeed, in need of help.

He closed his eyes.

"Go away," he said. "Please!"

The girl, frightened, started out swiftly.

"O.K.," she said placatingly. "*Okay.* Don't race your motor. I just asked, that's all. Jesus!" At the door, she turned back to him and said, "You're weird, mister, you know it? I mean *weird.*"

She was gone.

He made his way to the back room where he opened a drawer, reached in, and picked up a handful of ammonia ampules before proceeding to the office beyond. He cracked two ampules, put them near his face and took a deep breath. His head snapped back. He heard and felt a loud crick. He sank to his knees, stretched out on the floor, face down, and lay still for a long time.

He heard the bell, a voice, and after a time, the bell again. Dimly, it occurred to him that a customer had come and gone. He decided to rise, sent the appropriate messages, but his body would not respond. He thought himself paralyzed and was, in fact, suffering a temporary form of that disability.

The phone was ringing. He managed to make his way to his desk and answered it.

"Where were you?" asked Dr. Trask. "In the john?"

"No. Hello," said Freeman.

146

"You sound hung over," said the doctor. "Take a Benzedrine. That's what *I* do."

"No, no. Fine."

"Listen, then. Make up this prescription for colic, will you? I know you've done this one only about ten thousand times, but I'm making a little change in it for today —there was a piece in the *Journal*. Anyway. It's for the MacAlliney's baby—had a bad night, I take it, and the parents are in a state. God! They're babies themselves, damn near. It's getting to be like the old deep South up here. Teenage grooms and child brides. Anyway. Label it two-point-zero drops every two hours in warm milk as needed for colic."

"Two-point-zero drops every two," Freeman repeated, writing it down.

"Yes. The baby's only—what?—five weeks old. Here it is—the new version: Tincture of belladonna, tincture of paregoric, elixir of phenobarbitol, equal parts, twenty-point-zero c.c. each. Dispense in dropper bottle. Label: two-point-zero drops—"

"You've already given me that."

"So I have."

"Let me read it back," said Freeman, and did so.

"Right. Ted's on his way in from Chilmark now to pick it up."

Freeman looked up from his scribble and said automatically, "It'll be ready."

"Thanks. And take something for that cold, Freeman. *Anything*."

Freeman moved out into his back room. He began to work on the emergency order and concentrated well for a time, then felt torpor overcoming him once again.

He stood still for over half an hour, breathing deeply. The bell startled him.

"Mr. Osborn?" a charged voice called.

"Yes."

"It's me. Ted. Ted MacAlliney."

"Be right with you, Ted. I'm working on it."

He looked down at his work, realized he had stopped while in progress. He remembered now. The first two ingredients had gone in. Yes. There were the jars, left on the bench, as was his habit. He was about to continue, when he stopped. He was certain, still . . . His father's admonition surfaced: "There's a world of difference, son, between certainty and certitude." No. Play it safe. Begin again. He discarded the contents of his mortar and began again, slowly, carefully.

Meanwhile, from the store: "Doc?"

"Right with you, Ted."

Freeman was damp with nerves.

"Jesus H. Christ!" Ted shouted. "He said it'd be *ready* by the time I got here. My kid's *sick!*"

"Working on it," said Freeman steadily.

"Well, hurry up, God damn it!"

Minutes later, Ted appeared in the doorway, just as Freeman was typing out the label on the clacking old typewriter that had served the bench for years.

"Give it here," said Ted, picking up the bottle from beside Freeman's elbow. "It don't need a God damn sticker. I know what it is."

"Here, now," said Freeman, and snatched the bottle out of Ted's hand. He held up a warning finger. "Now, mind your manners, Ted. I appreciate you're overwrought, but I've got a responsibility, and you'd better

148

let me discharge it. Now move out of here while I finish."

Ted lost control. "I'm going to punch you right in the God damn mouth!" he yelled.

Freeman, trembling, finished typing the label. He then wet it, with a small sponge, affixed it to the bottle, and handed it to Ted, who began to run with it.

"Don't drop it, you silly little—"

The bell cut him off. He began to shake convulsively. It had all been too much. All day. Was there something he could take? A tranquilizer of some kind? What kind? No, he never had. Why start now? Home and some food. Had he had dinner? He could not remember. Lunch? When? He closed the store methodically and walked home.

At last, in the privacy of his bedroom, Freeman fainted across the bed.

When he came to, it was dark. The alarm clock in the room ticked noisily. He put on some lights, drank water, and considered calling Dr. Trask.

He walked about, from room to room. Upstairs and down. Finally he fell asleep in a chair in the sitting room.

He was awakened, hours later, by a strong hand clutching his shoulder and shaking him brusquely.

He looked up to find Dr. Trask standing over him.

"Don!" he said. "Lord, I'm glad to see you. I feel awful."

"Sit still," said the doctor, already taking a pulse count.

"Listen. Did I call you? Or not? I don't remember. Give you an idea of the shape *I'm* in."

"No," said the doctor.

"How'd you know, then? I mean, you're *here*."

"Pulse okay," said the doctor. "Let's go to the kitchen."

They did so, Freeman leading the way.

"Do you have any oranges?" asked the doctor.

"I think so, yes. Rosella keeps the place well stocked —maybe *too* well stocked."

He found oranges and extracted their juice, using the electric appliance on the kitchen counter. He poured two glasses and handed one to the doctor.

The doctor took it, thanked him, and sat down at the kitchen table. He motioned to his host to join him. Freeman sat down. They talked of the need for rain and of kitchen improvements while drinking their orange juice. When they had finished, the doctor spoke.

"How do you feel?" he asked.

"All right," Freeman answered. "That hit the spot."

"Blood sugar," said the doctor, frowning. "Freeman. There's trouble. And we're part of it."

"Serious?"

"Yes."

"Go on."

The doctor was having difficulty framing his next utterance. Finally he said, "The MacAlliney baby. It's dead."

"Oh, dear."

"Four-forty this morning. I was there, but there was nothing I could do. I got there at about three, but it was virtually all over. It struggled—life dies hard, you know. Pure instinct kept some life in the little body for quite a time. I was astonished it didn't give out sooner."

"Yes," said Freeman, "that is trouble. Ted?"

"Well," said the doctor slowly, "for the moment, I've got him locked up."

"Locked up?"

"In jail. I got Manter to lock him up."

"I'm not following this, Don. What're you trying to tell me? What did he *do?*"

"He threatened to kill *you*. In fact, he was on his way here when I had him picked up. He's beside himself, of course, but that's not the point."

"What *is* the point?"

The doctor, moving slowly, reluctantly, put his hand into his pocket and brought forth a bottle of medicine. Freeman recognized it at once. He had typed the label badly. Crookedly.

"This is what killed it."

Freeman was on his feet. "Now, you wait one damn minute, Don. I'll stake my *life* on that compound. I'll admit I've not been myself for a time, but it's made me *extra* careful. That one. I remember it. I started it, was interrupted, and—just to make certain sure—I threw it away and started again. So don't—"

"The medicine's perfect," said the doctor. "No complaint there."

"Well, then?"

The doctor handed him the bottle and said, "The label."

Freeman studied it, looked up.

"Directions?" the doctor said.

Freeman looked again. A spasm as he read: "20 drops every two hours in warm milk as needed for colic." He stared at the label, hard, harder. It went out of focus.

151

When it came back it read, correctly, "2.0 drops every two hours in warm milk as needed for colic." A moment passed, then wishful illusion became shattering reality. "20 drops every two hours in warm milk as needed for colic."

"Oh, my God," he said.

"We're both to blame," said the doctor. "Mine is largely professional, procedural. The Association, you know, frowns on telephone prescriptions. Unless absolutely necessary. And then only those containing harmless—well, *you* know. This is why. The possibility of this. You can bet I've given *my* last on the phone."

"But for God's sake, Don! I wrote down what you said, read it back, had it in front of me, so how can *you* be faulted? It's me. It's all me."

"No, but as I was about to say, yours is legal— technically, that is. I've got Coby Saltonstall waiting. Out in the car. I wanted to tell you first."

"You did it well, Don. Thank you. But why Coby?"

"He's your lawyer, isn't he?"

"Yes."

"Well, you'd better talk to him, then. I'm going to leave you now."

"All right."

"I can't tell you how sorry I am."

"Thanks. What an ending, eh?"

"Well, don't call it that. Not yet."

Freeman turned away, looked out at the back yard, and said, "Whatever happens, I'll never ever so long as I live prepare a compound again. How could I? Could I ask anyone to trust me? Good Christ, I don't even trust myself." He turned back into the room and said, "Don't you see that if—?" But there was no one there. The doctor had gone.

Freeman started out to the front of the house and encountered his lawyer in the hallway.

"Come in, Coby. Come in."

Coburn was tall and thirty and every inch a Saltonstall. He wore his celebrated surname like a badge. His thousands of hours of intense reading had given him, in addition to myopia, a permanent frown. He frowned when he smiled or laughed or made love.

He was not smiling now. He had, in the past two hours, gone through the thick, buff-with-red-back books, seeking the latest disposition of like cases. He had already telephoned one of his celebrated uncles in Boston for advice and was awaiting a reply.

"Coffee?" asked Freeman.

The question startled him and he said, "No, thank you," although he meant to say yes. He was dying for a cup of coffee.

"Let's sit down, then," said Freeman.

They faced each other and for a moment seemed to be adversaries rather than lawyer and client.

Freeman spoke.

"How bad is it, Coby?" he asked.

"Well, serious—but not a matter of life and death. Oh. I mean—."

"You mean it *is*."

"Depends. We'd better begin with A-B-C." He consulted a sheaf of notes and began. "Dr. Trask—he *did* call you at six thirty-five? P.M.?"

"I didn't notice the time, but he called me, yes."

"You filled the prescription personally?"

"Yes."

"Anyone help?"

"No."

"And the label?"

"I typed it. Not very well, I'm afraid, but I typed it."

"Now. For the crux. When Dr. Trask gave you the prescription—"

"Yes?"

"Did you write it down?"

"Wrote it and repeated it, yes," said Freeman.

"Including the directions?"

"Including the directions."

"Now I have to ask you this. Important. And please do remember, Freeman. This is not a court of law, nor is it an enquiry. You're not making a deposition and, in fact, we may want to change your answer later on—."

"What's the question?"

"How did you happen to get it twisted?"

"It was simply—"

"No, wait!" Coby said. "Please. Was the light bad? Your eyes? A lapse? Was someone in the room talking to you? I'm not trying to put words into your mouth, Freeman—"

"Yes, you are," said Freeman, and managed a small smile.

"No, I only want to demonstrate."

"Coby, thanks. You're doing your best for me, but it's a simple case, really. I made a mistake. We all make mistakes. Some of us are not supposed to. This one was a fatal mistake. Costly. It cost a life. I'm prepared to

154

take the consequences, whatever they are. Tell me, if you can, Coby. What happens now?"

"Well, unless the MacAlliney boy cools off, he's going to swear out a warrant. A complaint, actually. But in this case, the charge will call for a warrant."

"Then what?"

"You'll be arrested. Charged. Answer the charge. Remanded. Later on, a few months, probably—tried."

"Can't we cut through all this?" asked Freeman. "Such a waste. I did something wrong and there you have it. Why go through all these motions?"

"Because the law has to operate in its own way, Freeman, according to its own form. Besides. It's not so cut and dried as you think."

"Oh?"

"There may be extenuating circumstances, in which case—."

"Not a one."

"You may not recognize them. You're not a lawyer." He got up. "Listen. Could I have that coffee now?"

"Sure thing," said Freeman.

They went into the kitchen and remained there for two and a half hours.

During this time, they drank coffee while Coby, with practiced skill, elicited the moment-by-moment story of what had happened from the instant Dr. Trask had called to the time Ted ran out of the store.

He filled pages of notes. He wanted a case. He did not want to lose. This was not a case he would have taken voluntarily, but Freeman was a client and he had no choice. His plan to run for County Commissioner

155

was nearing completion, and he preferred to have not even a small black eye as he began his campaign.

By the end of Freeman's account, his face held his curious frowning smile.

"I knew it!" he said softly but exultantly.

"Knew what?"

"I've got a—. We've got a case."

"We have?"

"Damn right." He rose and as he paced the kitchen, it became a courtroom. "A respected old pharmacist gets an emergency prescription over the phone. He begins to prepare it. The patient—the customer for whom it's intended—bursts in. A sick child has driven him into a frenzy of nerves. He's impatient. He charges into the workroom and belabors the old pharmacist. Hectors him, berates him. The pharmacist gets rattled. The man grabs up the bottle—unlabeled. The pharmacist, sticking to the letter of the law, will not permit it. They struggle. The customer threatens to assault him. Physically. The pharmacist—very upset now, deeply agitated —hurries to complete the order. In his confusion, caused mainly by the boorish and impetuous man, he admittedly makes an error. He regrets it most deeply. Such a thing has never happened before—no, not for— how many? Fifty thousand prescriptions—get me the exact number, if it's impressive, we'll use it. A tragedy, yes. But in many ways, Mr. MacAlliney brought it on himself. A misfortune, of course. Human error. It must, in the circumstances, be forgiven. If this is criminal negligence, then I do not understand the English language. . . . Do you see what I mean? How does that sound?"

156

"It sounds fine, Coby. There's just one thing the matter with it."

"What's that?"

"It's bullshit."

"It's what you told me."

"I gave you the facts, son. You supplied your own interpretation."

"But it's *all* interpretation, Freeman. That's what law is. Top to bottom—how a jury interprets the facts—how the Supreme Court interprets a law. Professor of mine once said—and I've remembered it: 'The Constitution doesn't mean what *you* think it means. And it doesn't mean what *I* think it means. It means what a majority of the Supreme Court *says* it means.'"

"It means what *I* think it means—to *me*."

"Freeman, listen. You're plagued with guilt. Understandable. You'll soon be a defendant. But do me—and yourself—a favor. Be that and nothing more. Don't try to be your lawyer and the judge and the jury."

They left the kitchen and returned to the sitting room, where they both moved about, too agitated to sit.

"Coby, your case—our case is full of holes."

"Show me *one*."

"What time did Don phone me?"

"Six thirty-five."

"What time did Ted turn up?" asked Freeman.

"Wait. Here it is. Seven-ten."

"All right, then. Why wasn't it ready when he got there?"

"I don't know. Why wasn't it?"

"I don't know."

"Maybe you were busy with something else," suggested Coby. "He's not your only customer. You had other things to do."

"But I didn't."

"Then why?"

"I told you. I don't know. I started, stood there— woolgathering—when the bell rang, he was there, and I'd only begun. So I threw it away and started again."

"Do you often have lapses like that?" asked Coby.

"In the past month, yes."

"Do you have any idea—?"

The doorbell.

A few minutes later, Coby and Freeman, joined by Sheriff Manter and his deputy, Henry Weir, were back in the kitchen drinking coffee. Freeman toasted some English muffins and served them with sweet butter he had churned, and raspberry jam put up by Rosella.

Meanwhile, they discussed the formalities of Freeman's arrest.

"You'll be back here in an hour," said the sheriff. "I mean, he could hold you, but he won't."

"What about Ted?"

"They got a head doctor over from the Cape to talk to him. He was goin' on real crazylike. And Judge Whiting went in and saw him. Tough as hell he was on him, too. He told him. He said, 'The Doc may have done somethin' wrong, but you're doing somethin' wronger. He made a bad mistake—you're making a worse one. You can't go around threatenin' people's lives. I'll keep you in here till you're old and gray if you don't behave yourself and act like a man.'"

"Then what?" asked Freeman.

"He's going to hang onto him awhile, anyway."

158

They proceeded to the courthouse. Freeman understood little of the language spoken or the form followed.

In the end, he was remanded into his own custody, after he had sworn not to leave the Island without permission until a trial date had been set.

He phoned Jacqueline and Max, explained the situation, and begged them not to worry. He would keep them informed. In the weeks that followed, he did so, without dissembling.

He turned the management of the store over to Mrs. Petschek and Martin Stein. He had them advertise for a qualified pharmacist in the *Vineyard Gazette*, the *Falmouth Enterprise*, the *New Bedford Standard-Times*, and the *Boston Globe*. He could not help smiling to himself as he imagined Ollie trying to ask the forbidding Mrs. Petschek for three rubbers.

He and Coby met daily and talked. Coby filled one notebook after another with details, scraps of conversation, and scientific data. He was building a case he now believed could win him, if not an acquittal, at least a suspended sentence.

He was following—actually for the first time—the teaching of Professor Felix Frankfurter of the Harvard Law School: "Don't concern yourself with the possibilities and probabilities of what the *other* side may say or do. Just see to it that you prepare your own case so powerfully, thoroughly, and securely that *nothing* they say or do will be able to damage it. . . . And remember, too, that the first rule of cross-examination—the *first*— is 'Never ask a question to which you do not know the correct answer.'"

159

Coby had never before had the occasion to be so fore-armed, but this time, the weight of evidence was against him. There was no question as to guilt or innocence, merely of mitigating circumstance, if any.

Many things were in his favor, and he compiled care-ful lists: Freeman's long-standing good reputation in the community, his war service, his personal integrity, and so on. On the other side, Ted MacAlliney was still undergoing psychiatric treatment and was, clearly, a hysteric who might easily have upset anyone and caused error.

Coby's confidence became stronger as his case gained in power.

As the days and the meetings went on, however, one area revealed itself more and more as the weak spot: that blasted thirty-five minutes between Trask's call and Ted's arrival. What *had* Freeman been doing? Why *hadn't* he gone to work on the prescription? No matter how many times he was asked, or in what form, his answer was a consistent "I don't know."

Coby had learned that those three words, on the wit-ness stand, were generally negative. They made the witness look, at best, uninformed; at worst, stupid. Further, this response too often suggested evasion.

He had no intention of asking any question that would elicit this answer, but what if the prosecutor did? Never mind, he thought, following the rule. To hell with the rule! What *if?* His adversary, County Prosecutor Stan-ley Willoughby, was a tired old man on the verge of re-tirement. The thirty-five-minute delay was a small point and in all probability would not come up. Don't *count* on that! Be thorough! he exhorted himself. But no amount of probing, no deviousness, no bullying resulted in anything more than that soggy, useless "I don't know."

One morning at six, while Coby was clamming on a sandbar off Eel Pond, a completely new tack occurred to him.

He had been digging and found that in this particular spot, it was necessary to dig deeper. When he did so, the clams turned up.

Working on the case, he found that almost everything was grist to his mill. His experience on the Eel Pond sandbar conveyed to him the idea that he must dig deeper. But how?

Later that morning, showering, he turned the hot spray into cold, as was his habit. He turned to take the flow on the back of his neck, yelled (as he always did at this point, waking his wife), and all at once saw it plain. Deeper, in time, meant *earlier*. Days and months and years pile up. The earlier ones are closer to the bottom. Deeper.

Dressing, he recalled Frankfurter again: "You've got to prepare from the beginning with the difficulty of never knowing, in advance, exactly where the beginning *is*. That's part of your job—to find the beginning."

He decided, on the way to his meeting with Freeman, to say nothing of his new-found spur. It might intensify the inborn New England reticence that was already sufficiently in the way.

Freeman was becoming restless, and suggested a drive to somewhere.

"Where?" asked Coby.

"Anywhere. And *do* something while we talk. All

this sitting and jawing. My butt's beginning to complain."

"All right, Freeman, but I'm not dressed for a boat or clamming. Anyway, I've *been* clamming."

"That so?"

"This morning. Eel Pond. Took about half a bushel."

"Come along," said Freeman abruptly, happily. "I'll take you somewhere."

They stopped to buy fruit and ale, then drove up-Island through the morning mist along the Middle Road.

As they bore left at Chilmark, Coby lit his pipe and asked, "Where we going?"

"Gay Head."

"Good Lord!"

"Why?"

"I haven't been out there in years."

"That's *your* loss," said Freeman.

"What's out there?"

"A place of mine."

Coby laughed. "Better not let the Edgartown selectmen find that out. You'll be hung from the yardarm for treason."

As they made the turn to Squibnocket Pond, Coby said, "Holy Smoke! I know this place. We camped out here when I was a Scout. Used to lie awake all night hoping the Indians from Gay Head would swoop down and attack."

"That so?"

"They never did, though," said Coby.

The mist, which had been slowly rising, had stayed, caught, here in Freeman's wood.

They walked about, Freeman outlining the boundaries of his property, and settled at length on the peak of the knoll.

Coby was properly surprised when Freeman threw open a camouflaged hatchdoor, under which lay a metal trunk-sized box. He opened it with a key from his ring and brought out a picnic basket, tablecloth, napkins, plates, utensils, and a small wicker basket containing several bottles of liquor.

They drank Wild Turkey and water, while Freeman lit the Sterno stove, heated a can of Friend's Baked Beans, and prepared sandwiches (tinned brown bread, deviled ham, peanut butter).

The ale was kept cold in the spring until needed.

"This is great," said Coby. "Now if only those damned Indians would finally come!"

"I love it here," Freeman said softly.

"Had it long?"

"Going on forty years."

"Wow. You must have a neat capital gains situation going for you."

"This land," Freeman said tightly, "is *not for sale.* Will *never* be for sale."

"What are you going to do with it? Anything?"

"Yes," replied Freeman. "Something."

Deeper, thought Coby in the long pause that followed. Earlier. Where? From the time Freeman came home from the war? No. That's not the way. Work your way backward from where you are. Where are you? He opened his briefcase and studied his notes.

Freeman, meanwhile, poured himself another Wild Turkey (strong, Coby noted) and drank it in a long, slow, contented draught. He loosened his collar and lay back, his hands cradling his head. He studied the rolling mist as it journeyed through the treetops.

Coby found a beginning. *His* beginning. The present beginning.

"Can we start?" he asked.

Freeman did not reply. He was in another time, although not another place. Moments, sights, sounds, aromas, tastes were being summoned up from his memory. Sheila was here with him. She was, even in death, as much a part of this spot as the earth or growth or sky. She was in the mist. He saw her, naked in the pool; lying below him, beside him. He felt her moving, with nature, above him.

"Freeman!"

The sound of his name, spoken loudly and sharply, broke his reverie. He sat up and looked bemusedly at Coby.

"Yes?" he asked.

"Sorry," said Coby. "Were you asleep?"

"No."

"And you didn't hear me? I called you, pretty loudly."

"Why, yes. I answered, didn't I?"

"The fourth time."

"Think of that," said Freeman, and reached for an apple.

"Freeman, listen. This could be important. Extremely. Has that always been a habit of yours? Going off like that? Into yourself?"

"No."

"But you did it just now," Coby insisted. "And after Trask called."

164

"Yes."

"Any other times?"

"I suppose so, yes."

"Can you recall specifically?"

"Coby. Be reasonable. You're asking me to remember not remembering."

"Yes. So I am. But if you do it all the time, how can you say, no, it isn't a habit?"

"What're you getting at? If you tell me, maybe I can help. This way it's like charades, which, by the way, I never *could* abide."

Coby continued gravely. "We may have to explain that thirty-five-minute lapse. Once you're into criminal negligence, any little thing can feed it. A jury is people, not experts. And they're constantly putting themselves in the plaintiff's place—or in the defendant's. O.K. Say it's me. My kid is sick. Doctor says, 'Right. Rush to the drugstore, pick up medicine. I'll phone the prescription. It'll be ready when you get there.' I get there. It *isn't* ready. Now, that isn't criminal negligence—but it *is* negligence. Unless we can explain the thirty-five minutes."

"I see."

"How long, normally, would it take to make up that prescription?"

"Ten minutes," said Freeman.

"Oh, hell."

"Why?"

"It couldn't take any longer?"

"It couldn't take *me* any longer."

"Here's what I was hoping: You're an inventor, a scientist, isn't that so?"

165

"No."

"You invented a substance that's become a standard pharmaceutical product."

"Thank you. But that doesn't make me an inventor. I'm a chemist by training. A pharmacist by trade. I simply applied what I knew and experimented, and luckily came up with it."

"But didn't it take a lot of thinking?"

"Yes."

"There you are."

"Where?" asked Freeman.

"We can *use* that. Anyone understands that creative people go off into the clouds once in a while. We forgive them for it."

"Sorry. That's not how it's been with me." He looked away. "It's only in the last five weeks and three days—that I've had these—what did you call them? Lapses."

Coby pounced. "Why five weeks and three days?"

Freeman stood up and walked away. He returned in about five minutes and said, "Get onto something else, Coby. There are certain matters I'm not going to talk about."

Coby stood up and spoke harshly for the first time in their long alliance. "Now listen, Freeman. I've taken this on and it's my job to keep you out of jail."

"But if—"

"Wait a minute! I've not finished. Just keep still till I finish. Don't get touchy about questions. And don't hold back. Not from me. I'm your lawyer. You seem to forget that. The fact that you tell me something doesn't mean we're going to use it—doesn't mean it'll go any further. You and I are in a privileged relationship. I can help you best if I know everything. Everything germane, that is. Let *me* decide what to use and what not, will you? If you don't trust me—don't trust me *completely*—then get another lawyer. There'll be a *lot* of questions pretty soon and they won't be submitted for approval, either. Once you've been sworn in and you're under oath—you've got to answer any question you're asked."

"No, I don't," said Freeman.

"Let me rephrase that. Any question the judge allows."

"No, I don't," said Freeman.

"Jesus Christ!" Coby shouted. "You really are one stubborn old bastard. I'm trying to tell you—. Look. If you go to a doctor, don't you tell him everything?"

"That's different," said Freeman. "You called me a stubborn old bastard, you know that?"

"I'm sorry. I apologize."

"No need. Actually it was only the 'old' that hurt."

Coby, unwittingly imitating Freeman, walked into the wood. He re-emerged to find Freeman sitting down, having still another drink.

"Join me?" asked Freeman.

"No, thanks. I've had more already today than I'm used to."

"Let's go on," said Freeman. "I'll try to be more helpful."

Coby sat down. He saw that Freeman was beginning to show the effects of the drinks. Was it unethical to take advantage of his condition? No. It was entirely in his own interest. What about analysts and Pentothal?

"All right. Do you remember exactly what you were doing when Trask called?"

"Yes."

Coby waited. Nothing more seemed to be forthcoming.

"Well, what?" he urged.

"The telephone brought me to."

"You were asleep?"

"No."

"No?"

"No. I was in a state of shock."

"Where?"

"On the floor."

This was good, thought Coby. Might be good. Why the *hell* hadn't he dug deeper before? Had Freeman purposely omitted this important detail or was it simply an oversight? No matter. Use it. The man is ill, but trying to carry on—no—trying bravely (courageously? gallantly? valiantly?) to carry on, but because of his unfortunate illness, makes an understandable error. Talk about mitigating circumstance! A sick man, doing his best to do his duty. Sympathy there. Coby was feeling more and more secure.

"How long had you been on the floor?" he asked.

"Between ten and fifteen minutes, I should judge."

"Now, look. This may be a line of questioning, so be careful. . . . And what *caused* it?"

Another pause. Too long.

"I'm not going to tell you that," said Freeman.

Coby, with considerable effort, kept his temper in control.

"I told you, Freeman. This *could* be a line of questioning. You *can't* refuse to answer. You've sworn to tell '*the whole truth.*' "

"Well, you don't have to ask me that, do you?"

"What if *he* does? Stanley?"

"Why would he? He's not going to know about it. Unless I tell him."

"Suppose he asks you what *I* asked you."

"What?"

"What you were doing just before the Trask call."

"I won't tell him."

"You have to."

"There are parts of this, Coby, that're nobody's God-damned business. And that goes for *you.*"

They exchanged a long, uncompromising look, the meaning of which was clear to both.

Coby packed his briefcase carefully. Freeman poured himself another drink. Straight, this time. He knocked it back as Coby stood up.

"Sit down, Coby."

"It's no use. Get someone else."

"Sit down."

Coby sat and tried to relight his pipe, which had gone out. His trembling hand made the effort awkward.

"I'm going to tell you," said Freeman. "And when I do, you'll see why I can't tell you. No. That's not— well, hell. *You* know what I mean."

"Yes."

"One day—a long time ago—1927—over twenty-five years ago, a quarter of a century, God help me— early in the morning—nine-fifteen—my life—it was the thirteenth of May—my life began. . . ."

He told, then, of his first encounter with Sheila, and

of the days that followed. He told of their first trip to this very wood, the location making the account unbearably graphic. He went on, his voice and his spirit gaining clarity and confidence. He grew more lucid as he continued, and by the time he was telling of their days and nights in wartime London, his account was perfectly organized and eloquently conveyed. He told of their plans for a future, of the idea for the Japanese house, of the various manifestations of their many separations.

He realized that he owed his discovery and his fortune to the fact that he had buried himself in work to blunt the pain caused by her frequent absences.

He grew cold and shivered as he considered, for the first time, that the physical condition which may have caused her death—the overweight and its accompanying elevated cholesterol count—was brought about by *her* loneliness and despair.

He recounted, without bitterness or self-pity, the many frustrations and interruptions and anxieties they had endured . . . their desire to spare others . . . the end in sight at last . . . the messages . . . their last, merry conversation . . . hearing of her death from Ollie, crudely and cruelly . . . the hours that followed . . . calling on her husband . . . the kaleidoscopic, unreal time . . . the funeral . . . the bikini girl with the cinder in her eye . . .

He went on and Coby did not interrupt until Freeman had brought the account to here and now.

When Freeman had been silent for some time, Coby said, "Thank you."

Dusk had fallen and the wood was dark as night.

They sat silently for an hour. The mist was gone. They put away the supplies and walked out of the wood to the car.

"So you see," said Freeman.

"Yes. If you could tell that, there's not a jury that ever was would punish you other than technically. As it is—."

"What?"

Coby shrugged. "It's a toss of the coin."

"What do you think will happen?"

"Well—"

"I won't hold you to it," said Freeman. "Just give me your opinion. As of now."

"All right. Let me put it this way. Right now, I'd settle for a guilty verdict and, in the circumstances, a suspended sentence. I think the revocation of your license will be automatic."

"Yes."

"And. No matter what the outcome of the criminal charge, you'll still have to face a civil suit for damages—by the MacAllineys."

"I'll give them whatever they want," said Freeman. "I don't see how anyone can put a price on a life. Who can tell what that child might have meant to the world?"

Tears welled up in his eyes as he spoke. Coby pretended not to notice them.

"What I've got to do now, Freeman—based on all this new—is figure out our plea."

"Guilty," said Freeman.

"Not so fast. Guilty of what?"

"The charge."

"Not if the charge is criminal negligence, for Christ's sake. Hell, no. We plead *not* guilty to that."

"But what's—?"

"I don't want to talk any more now, please," said Coby. "Or tomorrow, for that matter. I need time now to sort it all out. It's become another story. What I may want to do is sit down with Stanley and work out a deal."

"Oh, no—"

"Jesus! There's nothing collusive about that—done every day—it saves everyone time and money and wear and tear—he tells me what he wants and we may be willing to give it to him—without a lot of noise and hullabaloo and pictures in the papers—"

"Yes," said Freeman. "That would be good."

They drove back to Edgartown without further conversation.

XXIV

THREE DAYS LATER, Coby met with the prosecutor Stanley Willoughby. The meeting was not successful. Willoughby recognized Coby's desire to avoid an extended public trial, but as he was about to retire from office, a flashy trial and a dramatic conviction were exactly what he wanted.

Jacqueline arrived, and three days later, Max with the year-old Seth. Meanwhile, Jacqueline had engaged a nursemaid (a high school classmate).

172

Freeman showed them the letter from Colette he had recently received (sent via surface mail!). It read:

Dear Freeman,
I have heard news and I am sorry for your trouble. If you wish me to come there, I shall do so. There is nothing I can do there but if you wish me to come there, I shall do so. I am sorry for your trouble.
Accept my most agreeable sentiments.

Colette

He had replied at length via straight cable, to make sure he headed her off in the event she had second thoughts. Her presence here was the last thing he wanted.

He met a new Jacqueline, one whose existence he had never suspected. He had known a clinging, fretful child; a moody adolescent; and from her boarding-school days to these, a cordial but arm's-length friend. All at once their relationship was changed. Immediately upon her arrival, she took charge of the house and its myriad workings with strength and efficiency. She arranged with Mrs. Tremaine to come daily rather than three times a week, and engaged an up-Island girl as a sleep-in maid. She rented a second car and engaged the girl's brother to drive and shop and run errands. She had the New England Telephone Company install a second telephone line, with two extensions. She sent for Issokson's to come and pick up a load of long-neglected dry cleaning, and found a twice-a-week laundress in Oak Bluffs.

She did all this in order that she might be free to become familiar not only with her father's case, but

173

with the Massachusetts statutes that pertained to it. She appropriated all of Coby's free time; went to his office or had him come, again and again, to dinner and to spend the evening. On these occasions, their talk usually went on until 3:00 or 4:00 A.M. This did not keep her from rising at her habitual seven.

Freeman worried about it and warned her that she was unwise to rob herself of sleep.

"We'll sleep when it's over," she said, and went her way.

Freeman came to know Max, as well, during this time. Their relationship had been tentative, their meetings scattered. One busy weekend a few months following the marriage; a lunch in the Oak Room of the St. Regis, New York (during which time his mind was on Sheila waiting in the suite upstairs); a first-anniversary reception in New York to make up for the European wedding. Then, other than the time he had gone out for the birth of the baby, there had been little contact.

Now here was a new old friend. In the days ahead, Freeman would come to regard Max not as a son-in-law, but as a son.

Seth, too, was a comfort. Freeman watched him for hours at a time, thought he could see him growing. Often, as he wandered about the house in the middle of the night, he would look in on Seth. The sight of his grandson invariably made him smile.

Neither Jacqueline nor her husband made any attempt to dissuade Freeman from his planned course, but they made certain he was aware of the possible consequences.

During one of the long, incomprehensible wrangles in the courtroom, Freeman reflected that the tragedy had, in a sense, given him a daughter.

The trial itself turned out to be an apparently endless nightmare, not only for Freeman, but for his friends, several of whom were on the jury. It had proved impossible to impanel a group that did not include friends of the defendant.

Thus, by common consent, prospective jurors were not challenged on this point.

Freeman followed the proceeding attentively, but in time to come could remember only parts of it—the odd parts, at that.

He remembered that he had insisted on entering a plea of guilty, even though Coby assured him that the bill of particulars was so vague as to make this unnecessary. He could not recall, however, the actual plea or the reaction to it by Chuck (Judge Charles Eliot Whiting) or the members of the jury, although he was certain he had been watching them carefully at this point.

Both the MacAllineys had taken the stand, but this, too, had been blocked out of his memory. Yet he knew that in the lunch break following, he and Coby and Jacqueline and Max had gone to lunch at the Edgartown Cafe, that he had had a lobster roll with too much salt in it.

Coby said, "I thought it was significant that *he* cried all through his testimony and *she* was cool as a cucumber."

"Significant of what?" asked Jacqueline.

175

Coby was thrown. "I'm not sure—but significant. We'll find out later."

"Oh."

"He did and she didn't," Freeman explained, "because her brother gave her a glass of water with three drops of spirits of ammonia in it, about a half an hour before she was called."

"Now how do you know that?" Coby asked.

"Because Mrs. Petschek phoned me this morning from the store and asked because *they'd* asked *her*, and she wasn't sure."

Coby looked troubled, but said nothing.

Surely, Dr. Trask must have been a witness. Had he been? Freeman racked his brain but certain pages had been torn from his book of memory.

Why had he forgotten that, and not the ginger tomcat moving fretfully in and out of the courtroom, looking for a place to nap?

He finds a spot under the prosecutor's table, stretches, yawns, stretches and falls into a deep sleep, uninterrupted. A remembered line. "I love a cat. It doesn't give a solitary damn!" A play? A book? Chuck's gavel, signaling the close of the morning session, startles the cat. Awake, he sees the courtroom emptying, automatically follows the crowd, then, becoming aware that his room is being deserted, returns to his spot under the table. He is still there when the court resumes, but this time leaves with an irritated lope, as though escaping from a noxious odor.

Freeman was surprised at how little of his own testimony had remained with him. Of course, he could always consult the verbatim court record. He never had, although a copy of it lay in his file.

"State your full name, please."

That "full" startled him and caused him to reply, "Freeman Thaxter Osborn."

Jacqueline was startled, as well. She had never heard that "Thaxter" as part of his name, but recognized it as his mother's maiden name. He had never used it, although his high school diploma had been issued to Freeman T. Osborn.

"Where do you reside?"

"Cooke Street, Edgartown, Massachusetts."

"What is your occupation?"

He paused before making his considered response.

"I am retired. I *was* a registered pharmacist."

An objection. Sustained. He is confused.

Chuck looked down at him and in all friendliness suggested, "Just say 'pharmacist,' Freeman."

"Pharmacist," said Freeman.

It was all he could do to suppress a smile as Dana, the clerk, droned (just like in the movies), "Do you swear to tell the truth the whole truth and nothing but the truth so help you God?"

And his response (just like in the movies), "I do."

Was he in a movie? Was it *all* a movie? Or a dream? Whatever it was, it was certainly happening in black and white, not in color. This had happened to him before. When?

Coby was questioning him. It seemed a curious game, indeed, being asked one thing after another by a man who knew the answers better than he himself did.

Coby elicited the long story of his training and ex-

177

perience; of his apprenticeship; becoming a partner; assuming ownership. Then, his war service; his return; his experiments and their successful results.

There were objections to some of the questions, but not many. He understood that Coby wanted to make certain that, should an appeal ever be required, a portrait of Freeman Osborn would be a documented part of it. Surely, the jury was learning nothing they did not already know, nor was Chuck, who tried to conceal his boredom throughout this phase by leaning forward and assuming a listening look. To all who knew him, it was clear that his full energies were being used to keep himself awake.

Finally, Coby came to the crux of the matter.

"This brings us," he said, "to the day and the evening of the—the misunderstanding."

WITNESS: No.

COUNSEL: I beg your pardon?

WITNESS: There *was* no misunderstanding.

THE COURT: May I suggest to the witness that a more orderly record will result if he will be good enough to confine himself to answering such questions as are put to him?

WITNESS: Sorry, Chuck. I just didn't want there to be any misunderstanding—I mean here—not then. Then, there wasn't. None at all. I'm sorry. That's confused.

THE COURT: Yes, I'm afraid it is and it was for that precise reason I advised you simply to answer the questions. There is no need to volunteer information or to voice opinions. There are competent men here to get

178

the information we need, and the *opinion* is the job of the judge and jury.

WITNESS: O.K., Chuck. I'll do my best.

THE COURT: You may proceed.

COUNSEL: Thank you, Your Honor. We were on the point of examining the events on the day of the—mischance. Did Doctor Trask phone you at six thirty-five on that day?

WITNESS: On the day of the *mistake*, Doctor Trask called me at six thirty-five P.M., yes.

COUNSEL: May it please the Court: I must request a short recess for the purpose of vital conference with my client.

THE COURT: I should think so. Granted.

(Recess.)

Coby beckoned to Freeman, who stepped down from the witness stand, and to Jacqueline and Max, who came forward. The group left the room and went into a corridor behind the bench.

"I can't do it, Freeman," said Coby. "Not if you won't help me."

"Help you *what?*"

"Make a case."

Jacqueline spoke. "You've got to help him, Dad."

"I *am.*"

"No, you're not."

Coby said, "Not if you insist on changing 'mischance' to 'mistake,' you're not. I know what I'm doing."

Freeman's face flushed with anger as he said, "And so do *I* know what you're doing. You're trying to put a better face on an ugly fact. And I don't want—"

179

"Freeman," said Coby patiently, "would you like me to step down?"

"No," said Jacqueline, "he wouldn't." She turned to her father. "Dad, will you please—could you please just answer the questions?"

"No," said Freeman. "No, I couldn't. You heard me promise. You saw me try. But it's no good. This game goes against the grain. I know what happened and I don't want to hide any part of it—certainly not behind language that doesn't mean anything. Mischance, for Christ's sake! I know what mischance is, believe me. I've known it. I've known too *much* of it!"

His voice broke. He got out a handkerchief and blew his nose. Max went and got him a Lily cupful of water.

"Thanks," he said, and drank it.

Coby sighed and shrugged. "Well," he said, "I don't know *what* to do."

"Come on," said Freeman. "Ask away. I'll answer. Don't worry. It's all the same."

(Recess over.)

X X V

COUNSEL: Did Doctor Trask phone you at six thirty-five on the evening of the mischance?

WITNESS: Yes.

COUNSEL: Did he dictate a prescription for the Mac-Alliney infant?

WITNESS: Yes.

COUNSEL: Did you carefully commit this prescription to paper?

WITNESS: Yes.

COUNSEL: Did you then fill this prescription?

WITNESS: I did, but not—

COUNSEL: Did you or did you not?

WITNESS: I did.

COUNSEL: Was it absolutely accurate to the most precise degree?

WITNESS: Absolutely.

COUNSEL: You swear to that?

WITNESS: I do.

COUNSEL: What happened then? Tell us fully, please.

WITNESS: Well, what happened then was exactly the way Ted told it. I've got nothing to add or subtract.

COUNSEL: We'd like the account from *your* point of view, please.

WITNESS: I was typing the label. He came in. Agitated—understandably—at the delay. Anyone would have been. He grabbed the bottle, started out. I took it from him—it doesn't do to have medicine in blank bottles. We got into some fuss, raised a little sand. I finished the label, fast. I kept worrying he might grab it again—and he did, too, the minute I'd stuck it on.

COUNSEL: Is this the label you typed?

WITNESS: Looks like it, yes.

COUNSEL: Is it?

WITNESS: Yes.

COUNSEL: What's wrong with it?

WITNESS: The decimal is missing, so it reads "twenty" instead of "two point zero."

COUNSEL: Can you explain the error?

WITNESS: No.

COUNSEL: Might it have been the result of the altercation?

WITNESS: Might.

COUNSEL: How many such altercations have you had in your experience?

WITNESS: Four, including this one.

COUNSEL: Four.

WITNESS: Once, a customer—an old customer—tried to get me to give him a refill on a suppository order. I couldn't—it contained opium. He pushed me around some. Police came.

COUNSEL: When did this happen?

WITNESS: 1938.

COUNSEL: Can you tell us the name of this person?

WITNESS: Yes, I can—but I won't.

COUNSEL: Why not?

WITNESS: Because he's on the jury.

(Laughter.)

THE COURT: All right, all right. Let's hold it. This isn't a vaudeville show.

WITNESS: Another time was even before. Prohibition. I was the only store in town that had any whiskey whatever. It was labeled "For Medicinal Purposes Only." Fellow came in with a fake prescription—tried to get a bottle—when he couldn't—smashed up my whole damn—sorry—my whole back room. And broke two of my fingers.

COUNSEL: And one other?

WITNESS: Yes, a girl—but I'm not going to talk about that.

COUNSEL: Will you say when?

WITNESS: Yes. Just before the war. When we had several British ships anchored here and were doing what we could for the crews.

(Laughter.)

COUNSEL: In other words, nothing like this had happened to you since 1940—and you were stunned.

WITNESS: Yes. Upset.

COUNSEL: Upset. Thrown. Rattled. Disturbed. Perturbed. Unnerved. Unstrung. Flustered.

WITNESS: All those, yes. Except unstrung.

COUNSEL: How many prescriptions have you filled? I mean you personally.

WITNESS: Well, I knew you were going to ask me that so I looked it up. Thirty-three thousand, seven hundred and twenty-seven. Including this last one. The MacAlliney.

COUNSEL: Had you ever made an error before?

WITNESS: Yes.

COUNSEL: When was that?

WITNESS: My second year in the store—

COUNSEL: What happened?

WITNESS: I was in a tearing hurry and left out an ingredient in a cough compound.

COUNSEL: How was that error discovered?

WITNESS: Well, it was for old Mrs. Sheila—

COUNSEL: Go on.

WITNESS: Yes.

COUNSEL: Are you all right?

WITNESS: No. Yes.

COUNSEL: Do you wish to continue?

WITNESS: —old Mrs. Sheila Murphy. And she'd been

183

taking that cough syrup every night for about eighteen years and she could tell right off from the taste that something was missing.

COUNSEL: What *was* missing?

WITNESS: The codeine was missing. That was kept locked in the safe, which was how I came to omit it. I'm sorry. I shouldn't have said all that. I don't know what's the matter with me. Something. I—

COUNSEL: So we have a grand total of two errors in thirty-three thousand, seven hundred and twenty-seven prescriptions. Or thirty-three thousand, seven hundred and twenty-five correct out of thirty-three thousand, seven hundred and twenty-seven.

WITNESS: Pharmacists make very few errors. I don't consider my record outstanding.

COUNSEL: That's all.

Cross-examination followed. By this time, Freeman knew every inch of the case and it was clear to him almost at once that the prosecutor was ill-prepared. He had left the spade work to his assistants and, although he had lists of facts, his grasp of the case as a whole was so faulty that he was unable to relate them, one to another.

Freeman waited for the question regarding the elapsed time between the doctor's call and Ted's arrival. He was ready with his "I don't know" answer, but the question never came.

The prosecutor was polite—*over*polite. As the routine questions and answers came and went, Freeman reflected on this point. Coby had done, apparently, such an outstanding job of character building that the prosecutor was reluctant to lose the jury's sympathy by treating him harshly.

The prosecutor was making no new points, unearthing no fresh intelligence and throwing no additional light. Then, by accident (what Coby was later to call "dumb luck"), he stumbled upon a vital disclosure.

It came in the fourth hour of the cross-examination, at which point the jury, as well as the judge and the handful of spectators, knew each answer as each question they had anticipated was asked. Contagious yawns began a chain reaction.

The judge called a recess. Large amounts of coffee and Coca-Cola were consumed.

The questioning continued.

PROSECUTOR: Some time earlier this morning, Mr. Osborn, your attorney used the words "misunderstanding" and "mischance" and you said—

COUNSEL: Objection.

THE COURT: Overruled.

COUNSEL: Exception.

THE COURT: Proceed.

PROSECUTOR: —and you also used the word "mistake"—

COUNSEL: Objection.

THE COURT: Overruled. It's all in the record, anyway, Counsel.

COUNSEL: Yes, Your Honor, but my objection is to the undue, you know, emphasis given these vagrant— what do you call them—semantics.

PROSECUTOR: We all make mistakes, Counsel.

THE COURT: Proceed.

PROSECUTOR: Mr. Osborn—let me put it to you this

way: You have been well presented and represented as a man of honor and integrity in your profession as well as in your community. No one here doubts that. Not for a moment. There is no question of guilt or innocence—merely of responsibility—

THE COURT: Is this your summation or are you still asking a question?

PROSECUTOR: If Your Honor please, I want to make sure the witness understands the question.

THE COURT: What question?

PROSECUTOR: Well, one I'm about to ask.

THE COURT: Well, I suggest you ask it and if the witness fails to understand it, he'll say so.

PROSECUTOR: As you wish, Your Honor. Mr. Osborn. In the circumstances, how would you yourself characterize your act?

COUNSEL: Objection.

THE COURT: Grounds?

COUNSEL: We're not concerned here with the *witness's* opinion. You made that clear this morning.

PROSECUTOR: May I remind my learned adversary that I am cross-examining and that—

THE COURT: Why don't you withdraw the question? I'd rather not rule on this. Anyway, it's not important.

PROSECUTOR: I respectfully decline, Your Honor. The question seems to me absolutely and importantly relevant.

THE COURT: All right, then. Overruled.

COUNSEL: Exception.

PROSECUTOR: Will the clerk repeat the question, please?

THE CLERK: In the circumstances, how would you yourself characterize your act?

WITNESS: I would call it—criminal negligence.

Coby sprang to his feet, then realized he had nothing to say.

The prosecutor said, "Thank you, that's all."

Jacqueline and her husband looked at each other, dumbfounded.

The judge covered his eyes with his hand and thought things over.

The jury was confused.

What followed was not only anti-climactic, but largely meaningless. There were other witnesses, but their testimony seemed no longer to matter.

The summations came. The prosecutor's, brilliantly brief; Coby's, desperate.

He spoke of the anatomy of guilt, of the suffering Freeman Osborn had endured, and pounded at the legal point that they, the jury, were charged with formulating their *own* opinion as to the nature of the act; that Osborn was not competent in this instance.

There followed the judge's charge, in which the same point was made, although in terms less clear.

The jury retired and, apparently sensing Freeman's desire, returned in less than an hour to oblige him with a verdict of guilty of criminal negligence as charged.

Coby left the courtroom in a highly agitated state as soon as the judge had set the following morning for sentencing.

Freeman went home with his family.

Jacqueline and Max, now believing Freeman to be mentally disturbed, treated him with great deference.

187

Freeman mixed cocktails for all and joked about the juror who had kept falling asleep.

"I think," he said, "the two on either side of Everett would have corked off themselves if they hadn't been kept so busy poking at *him*."

Dinner was served, family style, everything on the table and passed around.

The food was discussed. The fine leg of lamb. Was it native?

"No, damn few lambs on the Island these days," Freeman said. "Loose dogs've been harassing hell out of them."

The mint? Native. And the exceptional tiny pea potatoes from Greene's Farm.

"Yes. A damn short season for those."

Perhaps they would go clamming tomorrow. What time?

Coby's empty chair was conspicuous.

Jacqueline asked Rosella to clear his place, but Freeman said, "Leave it. He'll turn up."

"No, he won't, Dad," said Jacqueline.

Her father proved to be right. Coby came in and joined them during the deep-dish apple pie.

"Sorry," he said, as he took his place. "I'm a bad loser."

The roast was returned and Coby ate heartily. Freeman got up, went out, and came back with beers for himself and for Coby.

Over coffee, they discussed the case.

Jacqueline asked, "What'll happen now?"

"Well," Coby replied, "the silly bastards haven't left

188

Chuck much leeway. All he can do now is go by the book."

"And what does the book *say?*" asked Max.

"He'll go for the minimum, of course. The one-thousand fine and the one year."

Freeman asked, "How soon could it begin?"

Coby emitted one of his rare laughs.

"Not so fast," he said. "We've got a long way to go. I've been at the office all this time, looking up a few things. Chuck made at least four mistakes—two small, but two big. I'd give the appeal a hell of a good chance. Plus which, I've already talked to Boston and it's pretty sure we can get the Massachusetts Pharmacists Association to file an *amicus curiae*—"

"What's that?" asked Max.

"You know—friend of the court. Interested party. I could get the national organization, but we ought to save them in case we have to go any higher—which, by the way, I doubt."

"We're not going anywhere," said Freeman. "At least, you're not. I'm going to jail."

"Dad!"

He went on. "I'm sick of all this. I don't understand half of what the hell's going on and what anybody's talking about. It seems simple to me. You break a law, you pay the fine. Or do the time. Then it's over. I don't want to turn my life into a long God-damned drawn-out mess of litigation. A year isn't so long—and, anyhow, wouldn't I get time off for good behavior? That is, if I behave good?"

"Dad," his daughter said gently, "why don't you sleep on it?"

189

"What the hell do you *think* I've been sleeping on?"

"Take it easy, Freeman," said Max.

"We're all on the same side, Dad," said Jacqueline.

"Sorry, Bunny," said Freeman, using her childhood name for the first time in thirty years. He moved to her, kissed her, and added, "I love you." He returned to his place, sat down and asked, "I don't *have* to appeal, do I?"

After a considerable pause, Coby, having relit his pipe, said, "No, you *don't* have to. But *I* have to."

"Oh? Why's that?"

"Because, Mr. Osborn, like you—I have a profession and a standing—and a reputation to protect."

"Is that so? I thought I hired you to protect me."

"You didn't *hire* me—I'm not a hired hand—you *retained* me."

"All right, then. Now I'll *un*retain you."

Coby, moving about, stopped in front of Jacqueline. "Can *you* get any sense into him?" he asked.

"Why don't we meet tomorrow?" Max suggested.

"You're being selfish, Dad," said Jacqueline.

"Yes," he said. "I suppose I am. And thinking about it, I conclude I've got a right to be. I'm not going to appeal—I even hate the *word*—'appeal'—!" He spat it. "Now, far as *I'm* concerned, it's done. We've gone through the motions. I'm going to take my whipping and try not to cry. Good night."

The three who remained sat until 4:00 A.M., talking, thinking, arguing, winding down—but knowing all the while that ultimately Freeman's will would prevail.

Coby, who had warned that he would no longer appear for Freeman unless permitted to file an appeal, did appear.

This time, the Duke's County courtroom was crowded. The idea of being present at the sentencing appealed to the many. It was like being there at the finish line of the regatta. It had the attraction of brevity. It was the nearest remaining entertainment to the public chastisement so beloved by their ancestors.

There were seven other registered pharmacists on the Island. Two who did business in Vineyard Haven; one in Oak Bluffs; one in Chilmark; one who had retired but kept his registry just in case, and sometimes served as a temporary replacement; and, of course, Mrs. Petschek and Martin Stein.

All of them came unannounced, uninvited, and sat beside Freeman throughout the proceedings.

Early that morning, Freeman had asked Jacqueline to phone Judge Whiting and ask if he was going to request a statement before the sentencing.

"Well, it's customary," the judge had said, "but I won't if he doesn't want me to."

"No, no," said Jacqueline. "That's just the point. He wants to make sure he can say what he has to say. He's been up all night preparing it."

"All right," said the judge, "but tell him to keep it short, will you? It's just a formality, anyhow."

The moment came, after what seemed to Freeman an unneccessarily lengthy charge from the bench. (No wonder Chuck had asked that *his* be kept short, he thought.) The judge reviewed the events, praised both the prosecutor and the counsel for their skill and lucidity and co-operation, then recited what amounted to an involved essay on the jury system. In certain cases, the judge maintained, it was not only proper, but ideal; in others, such as the one before us, experts rather than peers might better serve the cause of justice. The present jurors—conscientious and well meaning, no doubt—had either not understood or misunderstood his charge: especially that portion of it which related to the defendant's personal assessment of his act. He, the judge, had permitted the question on cross-examination although it would not have been allowed on direct. The nuance had been lost on them, he feared, because as laymen they could not be expected to follow the fine points of the law. Still, he *thought* he had made it clear—eminently clear—that the defendant's opinion was in no way conclusive. In his opinion, they had erred. In his view, after a careful study of the evidence and documentation, the defendant was guilty of carelessness, perhaps of malpractice—meaning *bad* practice, from the root word *mal*—that he strongly doubted higher courts would sustain the verdict of guilty of *criminal* negligence which, according to accepted legal precepts, requires a wanton attitude, surely unproven here. Still, the law was firm and judges such as himself were sworn to uphold it and to administer penalties whatever their personally held feeling might be.

"Now," said the judge, "does the convicted wish to make any statement before sentence is passed?"

"Yes, sir. Yes, Your Honor."

"You may proceed."

Freeman took some folded sheets of yellow paper

from his breast pocket, unfolded them, put on his reading glasses and began to read.

"I wish to state that I have never before been involved in a court proceeding and I have been greatly gratified to observe our form of justice in action. I believe that my trial was fair, the judge considerate, the jury attentive—mostly—and the witnesses truthful. The prosecutor seemed to me to be seeking no more and no less than the truth of the matter, and my own counsel, Mr. Coburn Saltonstall, represented me in the most exemplary possible manner. So much for that. I maintain that I made a terrible blunder, an unforgivable mistake and that, for this, I should indeed be punished. My regret and remorse and sense of guilt are, I fear, beyond my power to express. To the parents of the infant whose death I inadvertently, but surely, caused, I offer my abject apology. No term in prison can restore life to that hapless infant, yet I mean to serve it, as a reminder, I trust, to others of my calling, of how often we hold life and death in our hands, and with what unrelenting care and caution we must perform our responsible duties. . . . No amount of money, no material gain can make up to the parents the forever absence of their child, yet it is my intention, as a penance, to turn over to them a basic part of my estate. . . . The suspension of my license is, in many ways, the most painful part of this ghastly misfortune—yet I must accept it as just. I shall dispose of my establishment here and shall never again practice pharmacy anywhere. . . . My good counsel has recommended an appeal of this verdict. With all due respect to him—and to you, Your

Honor—I do not wish such a maneuver to take place. I wish now only to pay my debt. Thank you."

It took Judge Whiting almost half a minute to get his mouth closed. He was truly astonished. He looked at Coby, who shrugged. He consulted the marshal and the clerk and the state trooper on duty before continuing.

Finally, in no little confusion, he said, "This is, of course, most unusual—unprecedented, at least in my experience—one would have thought—that is to say, there *is* a usual procedural—. However. In the circumstances, it is my duty—strike that—my *painful* duty—to sentence you, Freeman Thaxter Osborn to a term of penal servitude in the state penitentiary at Walpole for a term not to exceed twelve months from the date of your incarceration, and to pay over to the clerk of this court a fine in the amount of one thousand dollars. . . . Since no appeal from this sentence is to be filed, I instruct the marshal to seize the prisoner at the bar, to place him in custody, and to transfer him without delay and with the appropriate documents to Captain Anthony Murillo of the Massachusetts State Police who is hereby charged with the responsibility of handing over the prisoner to the proper authorities. . . . Are there any questions? Is there anything further? . . . This case is closed. The court is adjourned." . . .

XXVI

. . . WATCHING AN EXCEPTIONAL SUNSET from the Falmouth porch, Freeman was remembering his life with Sheila and infinitesimal details of their love and of their lovemaking. Sexual intercourse had seemed to him always to be the most exalting human action. Had they been—Sheila and he—two parts of a single entity? Of course. Did this, then, explain the continuing sensation of his being something less than whole throughout his life without her?

Their exchange had been a living thing, filled with growth and surprise. He recalled, without strain, the exquisite smile that often suffused her face as they blended. Yes, and there were times when laughter, as well, was part of it. Their love and their lovemaking had been joyous.

"How do you feel?" he had asked her softly one winter's morning, after long love.

"Victorious!" she had exclaimed.

His throat had caught, only because she had expressed so succinctly what he felt, what he always felt at such times.

And, right to the end, they had never quarreled. Not once, in all their years. Well, once. About the mistakes in the Adlai Stevenson campaign. That wasn't a quarrel. That was a political debate. Very well. What does it matter now? What does anything matter? They had once discussed never quarreling. The St. Regis. Was there anyone else in his life about whom this was true? Why not?

The attempt to find answers to these two questions occupied him for hours.

Quarreling was probably a habit, he reflected. A contest. A set of symbols. A ritual. Like card playing or tennis or prizefighting. A game presupposes a willingness on the part of the players, an adherence to the rules. There are those who quarrel to win, others who quarrel to quarrel.

He himself had often enjoyed the ones with Colette. They made it possible for him to relieve himself of pent-up feelings, criticisms, statements, objections, and corrections. Moreover, he found that Colette, in her passion, invariably revealed secret, useful information.

He had had violent disagreements with his father, although, on the whole, they were fond of each other. He thought his father narrow in political views and mean in business. "Near with a dollar" was his town reputation. It was in these areas—or their extensions—that their bouts most frequently occurred.

Jacqueline, too, had often been an adversary. In her rebellious periods, she appeared to take perverse pleasure in finding her father's weak spots and attacking them. Freeman did not, as a rule, take these battles seriously. He considered them to be common parent-offspring adventures. Still, he mused, they *were* quarrels.

With his lawyers? Yes. And doctors and dentists and business connections and customers—even with the rector of St. Andrew's.

Never with Sheila.

The circumstance fascinated him. Once, toward the end, he had asked her (not for the first time)—.

The end.

The end. He had not known how near it was.

The end.

Was there anything he could have done to delay it, forestall it? No. Nothing. Nature is whimsical. What a word! Not only whimsical but unreasoning, cruel, harsh, insane, unnatural. What? Nature is unnatural?

He smiled at his twisted thoughts, moved back a few moments in time, picked up the thread of his remembering.

Once, toward the end, he had asked her, "Why do you suppose it is that we never quarrel?"

The end.

The end. Stop it!

And she had replied, "Because we don't have the time, my love. It takes time. Think how little we have together. Wouldn't we be foolish to waste any of it in bickering?"

"But suppose we *did* have the time," he had persisted. "What would we bicker *about?*"

"Oh, I expect we'd find something. What to do— when, where, with whom."

"I'd give in."

"Why?"

"Because you'd be right, probably."

"Yes," she had said. "Probably."

He is kissing her, in memory, for a timeless time. He is looking at her, into her.

"Were you a happy child?" he asks.

"I suppose so," she replies. "Although it's only now,

looking back, that it occurs to me. I had doting brothers, and we lived in nature—the best way, isn't it?—and were always involved somehow with the animals and crops and seasons. Food. I was thrown from a horse once, broke my collarbone." She laughs. (That laugh!) "I certainly wasn't a happy child *that* day—those days. . . . And the beginning of my womanhood—as the district nurse referred to it—that was *most* depressing."

"Why was it?"

"Well, it meant a very real separation from the boys. Of course, we were always aware of our differences—and interested, too. We watched the breeding—not awfully romantic, but enthralling all the same—and somehow we were all part of the same—well—team. Then it began—my new function—for me, but not for them. And all at once, I was cut off. On the other side. For a time there, we became strangers—suspicious strangers. That was a hard time—not enjoyable, not at all. But on the whole, yes—a happy child. Were you?"

"I wonder. I was an only—and my mother was gone by the time I was five and the old boy was a tough Yankee with pretty fixed notions. He had no ideas about what to do about a child, so he treated me like a grownup. And I guess I became one pretty fast."

"And when did you get onto girls?"

"Not until—my God! What a way to put it."

"What? I meant—oh. Honestly!" She is blushing. They are laughing together. "You know what I mean," she says. "Meant."

"Sure. Girls. Well, they were—well—just nice frilly things all through grammar school. In high school, though, they were nervous making, and the most im-

198

portant subject in the curriculum. Algebra just wasn't in it—or French or Modern European History or Current Events or anything—not even sports, unless it could be used for grandstanding. College was talk, mostly. At least in my day, my college. A certain amount of peacocking around. Bluff and bluster. Some experimentation. The rich fellows bought it. For the rest of us, a good many false starts and dead ends. Frustrating. The Army made it all real, finally. Soldiers do it. Quite a lot. They worry, of course, about time running out."

"Were you a good soldier?"

"No. A scared one."

She puts her arms about him. They stop talking. They continue to communicate, however. Their exchange becomes deep, intense, passionate. Later, there is talk again.

Freeman, looking back across the years, thought it remarkable how, without constraint, they had found themselves always able to express what they felt, to say whatever came to mind. Her complete openness was, to him, one of her most endearing traits. There were times when she would guide him, carefully and gently, into new avenues of exchange. There were times when he would lead and she would follow. They had owned each other, proudly, happily. . . .

XXVII

. . . FREEMAN SERVED SEVEN MONTHS, two weeks and two days of his sentence.

He found the prison experience not unpleasant, but

never conveyed this fact to anyone for fear of being thought capricious or arch.

He thought it odd that he was assigned, almost at once, to the prison pharmacy. Word got around speedily, in the manner of institutional underground rumor. A small-town druggist convicted of criminal negligence was now working up in the dispensary. Black jokes were made and proliferated. When one of them reached Freeman—"Next they'll be puttin' the counterfeiters in the *print* shop!"—he laughed.

On the whole, he found his companions an amiable enough crowd, although, for the most part, they were bewildered men.

Newspapers were easily available, and Freeman found himself reading them more often and more fully than ever before. The vast mosaic of human action and reaction they described was infinitely absorbing.

A headline on page three of the *Springfield Union* caught his eye one evening:

Senator Van Anda
Wed in Washington

Recently Widowed
Senator and Secretary
in Quiet Nuptials

Washington, Sept. 14 (AP) Senator
Thomas Van Anda (R) Ind. and Mrs.
Gina Martucci Roos were married here
today at the home of Joseph Alsop by
Rev. Arthur Lathrop of St. Thomas's

Episcopal Church, in the presence of a small group of friends.

Senator Van Anda, whose wife died a year ago, and Mrs. Roos, a divorcee, will defer their honeymoon trip until the Congressional holiday adjournment.

Mrs. Roos has been associated with the Senator as private secretary for the past fourteen years, since her divorce from Arthur Roos, Assistant to the Secretary of the Interior.

The Van Andas plan to reside here.

Freeman read the story; then read it again and again, after which he tried to read what lay between the lines. The images that assailed him kept him awake for a good part of many nights to come.

That telephone call in London. "Mrs. Roos, my secretary. She's going with me, of course." Of course.

In time, he was able to dismiss it from his mind. He would never know the facts. He must come to grips with here and now, with what was concrete.

He laid out a program of activity for himself and followed it rigorously.

Using the Old Corner Bookstore in Boston as a clearing house, he acquired, by mail, a library of current books about Japan. From the bibliographies of these, he found other, older titles and had Goodspeed's seek out as many as possible. During one month, he read through the collected works of Lafcadio Hearn, that transcendental oddity who was born in Greece, made his reputation as a journalist in Cincinnati and New Orleans, but died a Japanese (Koizumi Yakumo) complete with Oriental wife and children.

At Freeman's request, Jacqueline brought him, on the first of her monthly visits, a Berlitz course in Japanese, with records, a player, and earphones for privacy.

On another occasion, she brought him, as a gift, a red lacquered box—the size of two cigar boxes—containing Kanji cards: Japanese symbols and pictures on one side; the English translation and phonetic pronunciation on the other.

In between Jacqueline's visits were Coby's. There was a great deal to do. He transferred his interest in All-Off to the MacAllineys. Thus, they became wealthy in one day—by means of a single signature.

Freeman studied maps and travel books and guides. He made plans. His spirits were, all things considered, high. He recalled Rosella's saying, one day, "Seems to me happiness is mostly just lookin' forward." At the time he thought it a rustic platitude, but now he saw truth in it.

He sold the store to one of the Vineyard Haven pharmacists of whom he was especially fond, but retained ownership of the building it occupied and assigned its title to Jacqueline and Max.

He began to correspond with bookstores and print dealers in various Japanese cities, not so much for immediate acquisitions, as for contacts there for his forthcoming trip.

With a calendar and a date book before him, he planned seven months in Japan—a span of time equal to his servitude. A repayment, as it were, from the bank of time.

He misjudged the amount of detail involved and found that he had to acquire a larger date book.

He decided to use Thos. Cook & Son, having heard that their facilities in the Orient were superior.

Jacqueline brought him, from his vault at the Edgartown National Bank, a locked strongbox. It contained, among other things, notes and information he had gleaned from some of Sheila's letters. He went through them carefully, copying out each of the numerous references to Japan. He wrung from his memory as much as he could of what she had said to him about certain places and activities and persons. He sifted these and finally larded them into his itinerary. What he was going to do, he reminded himself, was to make a trip to Japan with Sheila.

In the fifth month of his imprisonment, he met Tomoyuki Saito, a fellow inmate.

Freeman had wandered into the recreation room on one of his rare visits. The Ping-Pong and card games and aimless chatter held little attraction. In a far corner of the room, he saw a trim young Japanese looking at the pictures in a copy of *Life* magazine. He hesitated for a moment, wondering if he dared try out a phrase or two. He approached the young man, who looked up at him apprehensively.

"*Ko-ni-chi-wah*," said Freeman carefully.

The young man giggled and said, "*Ko-ni-chi-wah*."

Freeman thought, then said, "*Watakushi wa Osborn desu.*"

"*Hai. Watakushi wa Tomoyuki Saito desu.*"

The young man rose and bowed three times. Freeman extended his hand. The young man took it awkwardly and shook it once.

They sat down. Freeman held up a palm, then got out a Japanese phrase book. The young man pointed at it and giggled.

After a time, Freeman put together his next phrase.

"*Boregurai koko ni imasuka?*"

"*Nanakagepsu,*" said the young man.

Freeman did not understand, and the phrase book was not helpful. Still, he nodded and went on. He would not have asked, "Why?" in Japanese—but the word appeared, and seemed easy to say, so he said it.

"*Naze?*"

"Because I took a shafting, man, *that's* why," said the young man in perfect gutter English.

"What?" asked Freeman, startled.

"They set me up, those skunks, and I fell for it. So they get the cake and I grab six."

"But Mr. Saito—" Freeman began.

"Call me Tomo. That's short for Tomoyuki."

"But your English—"

"What about *your* Japanese? It stinks, by the way."

They laughed together and talked for the forty minutes that remained of the recreation period.

Tomo was a Nisei, born in the town of St. Helena in the Napa Valley in California. In 1941, since he was not yet eighteen, he was sent with his parents to an internment camp in Utah. His three older brothers had been drafted and were serving in the United States Army, two in the Pacific and one in Europe. Yet their parents were herded into a bleak camp, kept under guard, and treated like enemies. It had not made sense to him then, it did not make sense to him now.

After two years, having reached the age of eighteen, *he* was drafted, and moved from the internment camp to the induction center at Fort MacArthur, and not long afterward, to basic training at Fort Benning, Georgia. He was not to know freedom for some time to come.

Since he spoke and wrote and read Japanese perfectly —a result of parental insistence—he expected to be sent to the Pacific; in fact, he tried for various assignments there. The classification system determined otherwise and he found himself in Brownsville, Texas, training—because of his small stature—to be a B-52 tailgunner. He admitted to having been terrified of that exposed bubble stuck onto the rear of the lumbering bomber.

The war ended before he caught a mission. At this point, the Army began to woo him. The occupation of Japan had begun. Bilingual men were as needed as they were rare. He was offered a commission.

"I tol' 'em to stuff it," he said. "The way they handled me, an' treated my folks an' all—my mother got arthritis in there—I tol' 'em to kiss mine and as soon as I could I grabbed my discharge. I didn't go back to the Valley, though, because I met this Joe in the service, see, and he—"

The bell clanged, signaling the end of the period.

Freeman and Tomo agreed to meet again the next night.

They did so and became friends. Freeman engaged Tomo to give him lessons in Japanese and got permission to use a room just off the library for an hour each evening.

"We'd make a hell of a team over there," said Freeman one evening. "I know all about the place and you know the lingo."

"Take me with you," said Tomo.

"Maybe I will."

And he did. It took a considerable amount of rearranging of his plans for transportation and accommodations, but Freeman thought it worth the trouble. He expected to get far more out of the trip this way than with pickup interpreters. He was not going to need guides.

Jacqueline questioned the idea.

"He's a good kid," said Freeman, "but he's had a bad time. Fell in with these birds who had an airport scheme. To get jobs around different airports and then—using the damnedest most complicated system of faked invoices and bills of lading and changing labels and marking cartons—they filched a lot of stuff. Then they got bolder and bolder and went too far—but they made him the fall guy—saved their own necks—easy, because he's Japanese and you'd be surprised how many Americans haven't signed the peace treaty yet."

"I'm one of them," said Jacqueline, and provoked a row.

But Freeman had his way.

He and Tomo flew to San Francisco, where they spent three days testing photographic equipment and tape recorders. Tomo was gadget-mad and Freeman found himself buying all sorts of equipment: binoculars and radios, portable television sets and electrical heating devices, watches and chronometers and compasses. He thought most of it useless, but it added to the sense of adventure. Freeman carried, in addition to his letter of credit, about sixty thousand dollars in traveler's checks, since it was his intention to try to arrange shipment to Martha's Vineyard of all that was needed to construct his Japanese house.

The flight to Tokyo via JAL was splendid, and Japan was again a revelation, a dream, another beginning.

Tomo was of enormous assistance. He was thoughtful and swift and possessed the valuable gift of somehow getting along with everyone they met.

Moreover, he was sensitive to Freeman's need for privacy and did not intrude. There were periods when they would separate for days at a time before meeting at the next point of their itinerary.

Freeman was seeing all that Sheila had wanted him to see. He was coming to know something of the strange and profound ways in which the Japanese spend their inner lives. It was all, he thought during a particularly beautiful sunrise, revivifying.

There was one extended side trip he wanted especially to make alone. It fell between his visit to the Osaka teak works—where he ordered flooring—and the planned three-day stay at Nara from which the important pilgrimage to the Horyuji Temple would be made. This great structure, Sheila had explained, was the original wood concept, the basis of all Japanese architecture.

The side trip was to a country inn, Mingei-Ya.

"It's where we're going to spend our honeymoon," she had said. "We *are* going to have a honeymoon, aren't we? You may omit the carry-over-the-threshold part, if you wish. . . . Of all the lovely places I've known—well—there's none lovelier. It has no class, no chic—it couldn't be more simple—but it's of the earth and exudes the good of life. Food and wine and comfort and conviviality. Human contact is so easy there, so open. There are no locks on the doors. People wander about, being congenial. Everyone does everything. The girls who make the beds in the morning play the koto and samisen in the evening. The chef paints portraits of the guests and gives them away. And the little valet writes haiku and recites them at odd times. It's utterly romantic. Life—not as it is, but as it could be, should be."

With this description deeply imbedded in his memory, Freeman's anticipatory excitement peaked as the Mingei-Ya date approached.

He carried no more than a single bag, his briefcase, a Minox camera, and a small recorder. Tomo shepherded everything else to Nara, to wait and to make detailed arrangements for the week ahead.

Mingei-Ya. Freeman was not disappointed. In fact, Sheila had failed to do justice to the place—a dream of beauty and atmosphere. As the first day progressed, it occurred to him that she might have done so purposely, in order that she might not deprive him of his own joy of discovery. Sheila. Had there ever been anyone like her? As he moved through the ancient rock garden, tears came to his eyes.

He sat in a diminutive teahouse built to hold no more than two. It had occurred to him that things in Japan were made small in order to accommodate the needs of its small people: beds, books, cars, radios, rooms, and meals. Already, most of the postwar youngsters were growing taller, a result of American-influenced diet, and the vitamin supplements that some called "Sushiban wo MacArthur Gen-san" (General MacArthur pills). Freeman reflected on the problems this condition might raise in time to come, and found himself talking aloud— not to himself—but to Sheila at his side. He stopped, mid-sentence, shaken and troubled. He left the teahouse and continued his walk. Why was he so disturbed? He had often found himself talking to himself. During the time he was working on his formula, he did it often. It had helped him. True, he thought, but that was talking to *himself*. Here he had been talking to another. To Sheila. Was he all right? Was this a sign of something? The first step toward—well, maybe not madness, but incompetence?

He sat down beside a clear, dark pool and looked down into it. His mirrored image stared back at him. Here he was: Freeman Thaxter Osborn, sixty-three, retired pharmacist, ex-convict, inventor of All-Off, father of Jacqueline. Former husband of Colette (alive); former lover of Sheila (dead). What was he doing here in this remote place? Another land, another world. He had come here because of Sheila. Was she here? Was any part of her here, other than that which he had brought in his mind? How was it that she seemed to be materializing all about him? Was it part of the magic of the place? Or was he, indeed, losing his mind? No. What, then? Fatigue? The strange food and drink? Or water? Something was affecting him strangely.

As he began to walk back toward the inn, his reason

took the upper hand. Of course. Sheila and this place were inseparable in his mind. How often she had talked of it! How well she had described it! She had created so vivid a projection of them together here that it had become real in his memory, even though it had never happened. He felt giddy again, heard the sound of her laughter—from where? Or was that a bird, unique to the region? The scent of Sheila wafted across his path—that well-remembered, unmistakable fragrance that was hers and hers alone—or was it these blossoms he, a flower lover, could not identify? His feet did not seem to be quite touching the ground as fantasy enveloped him again. Was she here—in some way? In some form? Was this a meeting, prearranged? He struggled to return to reality in the way that one tries to break out of a difficult dream. On the way out, however, he controverted himself with the argument that no less a personage than his academic hero William James had given serious consideration to afterlife communication; had, in fact, had his brother Henry journey from Paris to Cambridge, Massachusetts, to listen unsuccessfully for William's signals from the beyond.

He sat down once again, obliterated his imaginings, and rested.

Reality returned solidly, during dinner.

He sat, cross-legged, on the *tatami*, to the friendly amusement of the girls serving him. (Someday, he resolved, he would master the far more practical ankle sit.) He had consumed two carafes of sake with the delicate *sashimi*, and was now savoring the hearty, peasant *shabu-shabu*. He had not ordered beer, but here came the second of the beauties, bringing it in a small pail that instantly called to mind the picture of himself as a small boy, trudging home from Pease's corner saloon swinging a similar receptacle for his father's supper.

Come to think of it, he had not ordered *anything* this evening. He had come in, had been shown to a *teiburu*, had sat. He had been greeted at once with smiles and assistance and a steaming, jasmine-scented facecloth. By the time he had finished using it, the bowl of *miso-shiru* was placed before him. The sake appeared. His dormant appetite had been awakened.

As he reached, reluctantly, the end of the *shabu-shabu*, the manager, who had been hovering about, came to him, knelt, and bowed. He was about forty, spectacled, moon-faced.

"I greet you," he said in careful English. "I am Iwasa Ito, son of the owner. Innkeeper?"

"How do you do?"

They shook hands.

"May I join you for a moment, Western style?"

"Of course, of course," said Freeman.

Ito sat opposite him—in the cross-legged position. Obviously a courtesy.

"Is all satisfactory? As you wish?"

"Mr. Ito, I couldn't wish for anything more. This is heaven."

Ito, embarrassed, laughed. "Oh no! Oh no! Surely you go too far."

"Believe me."

"Very well. You are my guest. In any case, heaven is an abstract, is it not? When I first was taken to the Top of the Mark in San Francisco, *that* seemed to me like a heaven."

"What were you doing *there?*" asked Freeman.

"My father arranged my employment in the States. The Fairmont. Days at the university. Nights in the hotel. I was busy."

"Sounds like it."

"Mr. Osborn. A problem. My father, I fear, has misunderstood some of your correspondence. He understood that Mrs. Van Anda would be with you."

Freeman paused before saying, "No."

"Oh. He is *most* disappointed. He has exceptional fondness for her—for so many years. She comes here often, as you know."

"Yes."

"I, too, have fondness of the same degree. She is my friend, from boyhood. She has taught me my first English word—'lovely.'"

Freeman felt stricken, trapped. The moment of revelation lay irrevocably ahead, like a whirlpool in the rapids. It could not be avoided. He dreaded its coming, tried to slow time.

Ito went on reminiscing, laughing—but Freeman no longer heard the words. Now! he commanded himself. Tell him *now.* The longer you wait, the worse it will be. Yet he could not bring himself to convey the news. Not yet. What if not at all? He would be leaving the day after tomorrow. Perhaps he could, after all, spare himself—and them—the agony.

His attention returned to Ito, who was saying, "—and I knew I was in love. Yes. She was the first object of my love. I left flowers for her and wrote horrid poetry. She was the cause of my resolution to learn English— in order that I would be able to speak to her—I had not yet learned that in this matter language is not important. Tell me. Is she well?"

"She is dead," said Freeman.

The serving girls were clearing, chattering happily, and attempting to make contact in sign language. Suddenly, one of them became aware of the enveloping mood, touched the other's shoulder. They scurried away.

When, at length, Ito responded, it was with a phrase in Japanese that Freeman failed to catch.

He finished his beer.

"Please," said Ito, his face contorted. "When?"

"A little over a year ago. July 11, 1955. In Greece."

"An accident? She was so young."

"No. Heart. She was fifty-eight," said Freeman.

"I do not know how to tell my father. He is not well. It will break him. She was his link to America."

"Why tell him at all?"

"Do I dare not?"

"Spare him. Of course."

Ito rose. Freeman did the same. He did not want Ito to leave him. He did not want, for the moment, to be alone.

They moved into the lobby.

"A cognac, perhaps?" asked Ito.

"Well, something."

"Please do me the honor to join me."

Ito led him to a small room off the lobby, apparently his private quarters.

Like all Japanese rooms, it appeared spare and impoverished. An illusion. A cabinet was opened, displaying an array of bottles from various parts of the world. The black-labeled Jack Daniel's bottle looked like an old friend, and Freeman greeted it accordingly.

They drank for an hour. Instead of becoming drunk, Freeman became loquacious. He wanted to talk. It had been some time since he had done so. There was so much that had been pent up for so long. Now, a let-go tempted him and he succumbed. Who was the centenarian who explained the attainment of his majestic age by saying, "I never wasted any energy resisting temptation!"?

Freeman told Ito his story: of his first meeting with Sheila, of their almost immediate involvement, and then incident after incident, not respecting chronology, but only their growing together.

He was telling of England and the war years, when he found himself walking with Ito, arm in arm, following a flashlight's beam. The air was cool and bracing. He kept talking.

After a time, Ito said, "I respect your courage, telling me alone. Here, by custom, a death is always announced by two, a pair. We think it too lonely, difficult for only one."

A town. A shop. Snakes in baskets on a shelf. Was it happening? He had read of it, never seen it. The shopkeeper carefully removing a single snake, the flash of a blade, a gland pressed, a tiny glass filled with—what? Well, snake juice. Another glass. Ito, demonstrating, knocks his back. Freeman does likewise. Bitter. No, sweet. Bitter again. No chaser?

They are on the road again and by the time they approach the inn, Freeman feels himself sobering.

They are in the bathhouse of the inn. Four women,

two middle-aged experts and two young apprentices, scrub and rub, rinse and massage.

Afterward, small trays of food are brought. Ito explains that this is part of the Kaiseki cuisine, in celebration of summer.

One of the older women leads Freeman back to his room. His bed is a colorful mat, called a *futon*. The woman helps him into his pajamas. He lies down on his back. She turns him over gently and rubs the back of his neck. Now his feet are being massaged. He glances down to see one of the apprentices seriously at work. He relaxes. He is spent, physically and emotionally. He is asleep.

He is awakened by a delicate, intimate caress. He opens his eyes. On the mat beside him is the older woman, naked, her long hair providing an erotic covering. She smiles and touches his face and kisses him. She continues, audaciously and skillfully and aggressively —but only for a time. She chooses an inspired moment to reverse direction and becomes feminine, shy, perhaps unattainable. Nevertheless, she is attained. She spends the night, which alternates sleep with lovemaking. The absence of verbal exchange makes the physical language more intense and eloquent. Yet, it is all strangely circumspect. He thinks of Sheila, of course, wondering what she would make of all this.

At dawn, his partner leaves him. He sleeps until the young apprentice brings him a breakfast of broth, ginger-flavored scallops, and black tea. Later, she adds *mikan:* a sweet, tangerine-like citrus fruit.

Freeman eats it all.

215

XXVIII

He encountered Ito during the midmorning. Nothing was said about the previous night's extraordinary happenings.

They chatted pleasantly for a few minutes, Freeman gaining information about the care of the exceptional water lilies.

Ito said, "I have not informed to my father. As you have suggested."

"Good."

"But there is a difficulty."

"Oh?"

"Yes. He asks especially to see you before you depart."

"All right," said Freeman. "I can lie."

Later in the day he did so, but it was not as easy as he had thought.

The elder Ito sat propped up on his futon. He spoke. His son interpreted.

"You are friend to Sheila Van Anda?"

"Yes."

"How sad we are she did not come."

"She will come soon."

"Alas, I am near my end. I have hoped to see her once again. She is a goddess."

"I agree."

"Will you give her my message?"

"Of course."

"Tell her that in my last hours, among my thoughts were those of her ineffable loveliness; that although absent, she has helped to ease my pain. She was a true friend, that rarest of all creatures."

Freeman swallowed before he said, "I shall tell her. Goodbye."

The old man raised a hand in salute, tried to bow, fell forward, and cracked his head on the floor.

In order not to embarrass the elder Ito, Freeman, who had begun to understand "face," left the room as the son began to minister to his father. Five women, summoned by signal, scurried past Freeman through the corridor.

An argument when Freeman was refused a bill. He insisted that he wished to pay.

Young Ito threw open his arms in appeal and said, "My father has instructed me. There is *nothing* I can do. And, any case, it is small, nothing. As we say here, 'no more than a sparrow's tears.' "

They said goodbye after Ito had promised to come one day to Martha's Vineyard, and after Freeman had promised to return.

In the crowded train to Nara he considered that if for no other reason, the journey to Mingei-Ya had made this trip to Japan worthwhile.

In Nara, misfortune awaited him. Tomo had disappeared or, rather, had failed to appear. The hotel there (virtually empty) had held the reservations, but had had no word from Saito-san. Only fragmentary English was spoken here and Freeman was in trouble. He telephoned the American consul in Osaka and explained his predicament: He suspected that his traveling companion, a Japanese-speaking American citizen named Tomo —no, Tomo*yuki* Saito—had gone off with his belongings, including some fifty-one thousand dollars in American Express traveler's checks.

A whistle.

"Were they in your luggage?" asked the subconsul.

"No. I'd handed them to him for safekeeping."

"Were they insured?"

"No."

"Do you have the numbers?"

"Yes."

"Phone them to American Express at once, although I'm inclined to believe it's too late."

"I agree," said Freeman. "This lad is sharp."

"We'll do what we can, of course, but from your description, he'd find it easy to go underground. He's made his fortune now."

Freeman spent a day and a half on the telephone. He phoned Jacqueline, among others, to congratulate her on her earlier perspicacity.

"Come home, Dad," she said.

"No, no," he insisted. "I'm not going to let a crooked little pipsqueak ruin the trip of my life. I'm off to Horyuji."

"Where's that?"

"You mean *what's* that. It's a temple. Made of wood. I have to see it for my project."

"Dad—"

"I'll see you on schedule."

"But you're cleaned out. How will you manage?"

"Letter of credit, passport, and a God-damn friendly manner."

Jacqueline was right again. Although Thos. Cook & Son were helpful, Freeman was cruelly fatigued by the strain of the days that followed. He had to replace essentials and revise his travel plans. At the same time, he had to deal with attempts to track down Tomo: claims, forms, interviews, police. Finally, worn and low in resistance, he succumbed to the virus that infected his stomach.

He flew home—was flown home—in the company of a nurse arranged for by Iwasa Ito.

XXIX

JACQUELINE TOOK OVER in San Francisco. After a month in the hospital there, Freeman was brought to Denver where he spent three additional months in the hospital, and four more in a convalescent home. Jacqueline prevailed upon her father to remain in Colorado, since she was in the midst of a difficult pregnancy and would not be able to travel east for some time.

When Freeman left the convalescent home, he went to live with Jacqueline and Max, but could not invent a life for himself there.

Jacqueline's second baby was born by Caesarean section. Another boy, named Max, Jr.

Freeman returned to the Vineyard. It was changing. Television. Dr. Trask was dead. Fewer sails and more motors. Loud music. Motorcycles. Camping sites and condominiums. The kids were growing up and taking charge.

His sixty-fifth birthday came and went after a New York blowout with Jacqueline and Max.

The MacAllineys were divorced. Each remarried.

Freeman found himself sleeping more, drinking less, reading. Why poetry? It had never much interested him. Now it was somehow strengthening. He found that he enjoyed form.

Jacqueline bought him, for Christmas, an album of recordings of American poets reading their work.

"Although I must say," she said, "I can't understand your interest in it."

"Neither can I," he said.

"Then why?"

"Well, it's like Housman said a while ago—A. E. Housman—do you know his stuff? *A Shropshire Lad?*

'And since to look at things in bloom
Fifty springs are little room,
About the woodlands I will go
To see the cherry hung with snow.'

Somebody asked him—Housman—about poetry, and he said he could no more define it than a terrier can define a rat. Do you see what I mean? What *he* means?"

"No."

"Well, there you are. Thanks for the records. They're grand."

He sold his house and took a small apartment across from where Dr. Andrew Lucas, his physician now, lived and worked.

He bought a boat, a forty-two-foot Owen cabin cruiser. He took it once around the Island. He sold it. He recalled, laughing alone, the standard description of the two best days in a yachtsman's life: "The day he buys his new boat, and the day he sells it!"

He went often to Squibnocket Pond and meditated, waiting for the thrust of energy that would complete the action he had so long envisioned.

He planned another trip to Japan. Jacqueline did everything in her power to dissuade him. He knew he was not thinking clearly or correctly, but getting his own way had become the main purpose of his life.

In his suite at the Huntington Hotel in San Francisco, he told his daughter to save her breath, that he was going.

"But by sea, this time," he said.

"Why?"

"Because it takes longer, that's why."

Another hour of fruitless argument, serving only to make each of them cling more firmly to previously held views.

Resigned, she said, "Will you take someone with you? A nurse, a companion?"

"Marilyn Monroe," he said.

"I mean it, Dad."

"So do I."

"I could get you someone and I'd feel better."

"You and Max come along. It'll change your life. For the better."

"We can't. You know that."

"Then leave me alone. Bunny dear, you've got to

try and see it my way. Look here. I don't know what kind of father I've been to you—"

"First-class. The best."

"Well, maybe. The final score isn't in yet. But you know I tried, don't you?"

"Of course."

"And the one thing I tried to get you to be—beyond anything else—was resourceful. Independent. Without those things, you can't have dignity. Y'know, ol' Mark Twain said it once: 'Obscurity and a competence; that is the best life.' Well, I don't know about the obscurity part—I notice *he* worked pretty hard to avoid it—but the competence thing, by God, I'm with him there. Remember what a bore I was for such a long time about you had to learn shorthand and typing?"

"You certainly were. But I'm grateful to you for it."

"Sure. Even if you don't use it, you've got it. It's a skill. Gets you around. In. You can always make a living with a skill—some kind of a living. And that may lead to something else. Everything in life leads to something else. And there comes a time for each man—woman, too—when he's on his own. You've got to know how to handle that. Everybody ought to be able to make a bed—cook a meal—sew a button—bandage a wound—beat off a dog or an attacker—fix a toilet—shuck a clam—apply mouth-to-mouth resuscitation—there's no end to the things we ought to learn to do. The more the better."

"But I *can*, Dad," she said. "Thanks to you. Except beat off an attacker. I mean I've never had to try. Why is that, do you suppose? Not attractive enough? I've *tried* to be."

"You're the second most attractive female I've ever encountered," he said.

She questioned him silently. He shook his head. She touched his hand.

"It worked, Dad. It turned out exactly the way you said it would. I took the damned shorthand and typing and hated every minute of it. Even back then I was some kind of a feminist, and somehow I'd got the notion that office skills were a—*you* know—a road to subjugation in some way. But you were—as you say— quite a bore about it."

"Thank you."

"And that's how, after the awful time in Texas, I took the UNESCO job and traveled and met Max and found a life. So you see, you were right."

"You do understand then, don't you, why it's important for me to make this trip? And alone? Time goes by, more and more's done for you, you begin to lose your sense of resource. . . . Young kids, y'know. There comes a time you've got to let them take their first bus ride alone. The same goes for old fathers."

X X X

HE WENT OFF, ALONE, but returned with a companion: Gaisha Muto, an elderly, well-known architect who had accepted Freeman's invitation mainly because he wanted to see, before his life ended, the American work of Frank Lloyd Wright.

From San Francisco, they set out for the East Coast in a Carey Cadillac with two drivers, making dozens of side trips during which Muto studied and photographed hundreds of Wright structures. They went to Spring Green, Wisconsin, and spent two days with the great master—a fortunate visit, as it happened, since Wright died a few months later.

All in all, the cross-country trip took them five months.

It was during this excursion that Jacqueline began to have further concerns about her father's mental state. She and Max consulted a close friend, Gary Feld, who was in psychiatric practice.

They had compiled a list of the many odd, unexplainable plans and activities in which Freeman was or had been involved since the MacAlliney tragedy: the trips to Japan, buying and shipping back masses of materials; the involvement with Tomo; the plans for building the Japanese house; the transfer of a fortune to the MacAllineys; and, earlier, the seven thousand dollars to Diana Boyle, a stranger; his new interest in poetry— the list went on and on. Looking for trouble, they had found it. It escaped them that they had picked out only strange actions and that the normal ones outweighed these.

Dr. Feld analyzed the material and suggested that Freeman was suffering from the complications of deeply felt guilt. This explained his profligacy and his desire to rid himself of his money. In the circumstances, he thought, considering the man's age and actions, he could very well be committed, at least for observation.

Jacqueline rejected the idea. But the following summer, she invited Dr. Feld and his wife to spend two weeks on the Island with her and Max. During this time, she arranged several events that gave Feld an opportunity to study her father.

One of these took place at Squibnocket Pond, where Freeman and Mr. Muto described the plans for the house and garden that were soon going to be built there. Freeman had brought out his two grandsons to show them Squibnocket Pond. They were impressed.

Later that night, over beers with Jacqueline and Max, Feld said, "Beats me. He could pass any test ever devised and yet I'd swear he's a bit off."

"About the tests," Max said. "How do you know?"

"Because," said Feld, "I've given him the larger part of three."

"You have?" Jacqueline asked.

"Of course. In talk. In questions. Did you think I was that interested in the dimensions and stresses and strains? Or the bird comparisons? Or the color identifications? Or the dates or times, or what day of the week it was when they saw Frank Lloyd Wright?"

Max and Jacqueline may not have been aware of Feld's method, but Freeman, discussing him the next day said, "Nosy sonabitch, that Feld, isn't he? Or is he giving me a secret sanity test?"

Ten days later, however, when the Felds had gone, Freeman called on Jacqueline and Max. They sat out on the back porch.

"I've given it up," he said. "The house. For now, at least. Gaisha tells me it would take three years or more to get it right. And he's worried about the craftsmen. It's a whole different ball game. We could—sure—bring a crew of ten or fifteen over, I suppose. But that really *would* be crazy, wouldn't it?"

"Yes," said Jacqueline.

"No," said Max. "Hell, no! Not if you want to do it."

"Max!" Jacqueline was stunned.

"Sorry, puss. I'm on *his* side. We've meddled enough. Dad, tell us to mind our own damned business. If you want to build a Japanese house on Squibnocket Pond, go ahead and do it. I'm sure you've got a good reason."

There was a long silence. Jacqueline left the porch and came back ten minutes later, carrying a tea tray.

In her absence, nothing had been said. Now, they all drank tea and munched on her blueberry muffins.

"Yes," said Freeman. "I *have* got a good reason. The most important reason in the world. In my life." They waited. "But I'm not going to tell you what it is. I can't. Believe me. I've got to do it before I die. What I mean is, I can't die until I do it. I don't *want* to and I'm not *going* to!"

"All right, Dad," said Jacqueline. "Don't get excited. More tea?"

Gaisha Muto returned to Japan, and the river of time flowed on for Freeman.

XXXI

ONE CHRISTMAS, he said to Jacqueline, "I never cared much for Christmas. Too artificial. But I'm glad of it now. It's one of the few times I'm sure of. I mean I know it's where it is."

"Yes, Dad," said Jacqueline quietly.

"Otherwise, these days I hardly ever know what day it is. Or what month. I ask people and they tell me, but even *that* gets to be confusing. I asked Doctor Andy one day what day it was, and he said Friday. So I went downtown to get a *Gazette* and when I got there, Irving said, '*Gazette?* Why, I'd've thought you'd know by now it comes out only Fridays in the wintertime.' 'Well, this *is* Friday, you ol' coot,' I tell him. And he says, 'I'll give you a good bet it's Monday.' Well, I got back and said to Andy, 'It's Monday,' 'I know that,' he says. 'Well, if you do, why the hell'd you tell me it was Friday?' 'I told you it was Friday last Friday,' he says. 'You didn't ask me today!' Well, y'know, things like that can make you real nervous."

"I should think so. And yet, don't worry about it. Easy to understand in a way. All your days are pretty much alike, aren't they?"

"Yes, but then the seasons. I get *them* mixed up, too. Do you suppose the time has come?"

"What time?"

"The coming unglued?"

"Not a chance, Dad."

There came a lengthy period when Freeman found he was sleeping by day and walking around or reading by night. How had this reversal taken place, and when? He could not remember. It took him months to return to normal routine.

A year or so later, a new problem involving his memory arose. He discussed it with no one. The fact was, he was increasingly vague as to certain of his memories. Were they of events that had actually taken place, or merely unfulfilled wishes and dreams that had become, by repetition, a part of his remembrance?

His attempts to find his way through the labyrinth of images and sounds perplexed him and often led to severe headaches.

In lucid periods, he realized that he was living too frequently in a state of disorientation.

He spent nights, sometimes whole days, in reminiscence. Their first visit to the pond. Yes. That had happened, he was sure of it. Tanglewood. Had they gone there together or only talked about it, planned it? The latter. London. Of course. All that *had* happened. Had they been together in Japan? Yes. No. No? What about their honeymoon at Mingei-Ya? No. But he remembered love, lovemaking at dawn. No. That was something else. They had never been in Japan together. Strange. How did *that* happen? Not happen. He got out of bed, found that he was as drenched as if he had stepped out of the shower. He took a shower, changed his pajamas, went back to bed.

Winters. Driving to Florida, alone. Sarasota: circus rehearsals. Delray Beach: visiting Island friends. Sani-

228

bel Island: collecting sea shells. Tampa: shuffleboard. And everywhere, going into drugstores and supermarkets and beach shops to make sure they carried All-Off. Invariably, they did. Seeing people using it becomes a never-diminishing thrill. Driving back to the Island. Hitchhikers. New kinds of people. The Chappaquiddick tragedy. A presidential election. Television finally captures him and he sits, hypnotized, days and nights. The "Today" show. Daytime serials. Game shows. News. Movies. War movies. Interesting programs on Channel Two. Early morning classes on the "21-inch Classroom." Talk shows. Funny stuff. The performers grow older, then old before his eyes, and are replaced by younger, louder ones.

Jacqueline bore another son. Named, at last, Freeman Osborn Tarloff. More like it. This one was Freeman's favorite. Bright as a button.

Freeman was living now in two rooms at the Daggett House and owned four television sets—all color, except the tiny Sony he kept beside his bed. Life had become a spectator sport.

The record player. The music of Charles Ives. Great stuff, he thought, before its time.

He found himself standing, one afternoon, in the entry of the main dining room of the Harborside Inn. He looked about, thought hard, then ran his tongue over his teeth, seeking particles. He tasted his gums. Face it. Ask.

"Have I had lunch yet?" he asked the headwaiter.

The headwaiter laughed. "You serious?" he asked.

"Yes, I am," said Freeman. "I don't know if I'm on

229

my way in or on my way out. And I'd like you to tell me."

He seemed close to anger.

The headwaiter touched his upper arm and said, "Your table's ready now, Mr. Osborn."

"Thank you."

He followed the headwaiter to a corner table, ordered lobster salad, rye toast, and iced coffee.

He lunched quietly while he worked out a new plan.

He went to his room, packed a bag, and called a taxi. He went to the airport and waited for the first plane out to Boston. It proved to be an Executive Airlines flight. He was the sole passenger on the small plane. At Logan Airport, he bought passage from Boston to Denver, and telephoned Jacqueline.

"I'm on my way to see you, if that's all right," he said.

"What is it?"

"Don't be alarmed. I'm phoning ahead because I didn't want to walk in and startle you. I'm in good health, but I want to see you. And Max."

They met him at the Denver airport.

"Let's go somewhere and eat," he said. "I'm starving. Can't eat that airplane muck."

"All right," said Max.

"Someplace jolly. Is there a place with music? Or dancing girls? You know, some kind of a night club? It doesn't *have* to be topless, but on the other hand—."

"Yes," said Max. "Several. I couldn't vouch for the food, though."

"I don't care," said Freeman. "I'm not very hungry."

Jacqueline and Max exchanged a look. Hadn't he just said, "I'm starving"?

They went to Laffite. The music was loud, the entertainment raucous, and the steaks surprisingly good. Cocktails. Draught beer. Brandies.

"This is fine," said Freeman. "Perfect."

When they got home, he said, "We'll talk in the morning."

"Why not now?" Jacqueline asked.

"Because you're drunk," said Freeman, and went to his room.

After breakfast and a visit with the children, they assembled in Max's study.

"Don't take any calls," said Freeman. "This is it. Important."

He told them of the incident at the Harborside Inn.

"I think that does it," he said.

"Does what, Dad?" asked Jacqueline. "I don't follow."

"I've got to make other arrangements. I've gone—cuckoo, we used to call it. Do you still?"

"You're not cuckoo," said Max. "You may be over-fatigued, or having blood-supply-to-the-brain trouble, and there's effective treatment now for that. Or something else."

"*Whatever* I am," Freeman insisted, "I'm not right. And I need looking after. I don't trust myself any more."

"Dad—" Jacqueline whispered.

"Now, the thing I'd like to avoid," he continued, "is being institutionalized. I wouldn't like that. I'd go mad." He laughed. "That is, if I'm not already. I'm told there are several fine retirement homes over on the Cape. I hate leaving the Island, but we don't have one there. I want you to pick one and set me up there.

231

Then, more important, I'm calling Coby later in the day to arrange the documents. I don't know what they're called, but I'm turning everything over. The fact is, I'm not competent. Not any more. So you'll have to manage things."

Jacqueline was weeping softly.

"Whatever you say, Dad," said Max.

"Don't cry, Bunny. I've had a good life—you—lately Max—and a great love. I'll tell you about it some-day. When you come east. I couldn't tell you here. She's part of there. So you see, I'm far more fortunate than most."

XXXII

THE STACK OF MORNING PAPERS was brought to Freeman's room with his breakfast at the Falmouth Sunset House. He had, of late, taken to reading ten or more newspapers daily. The *New York Times*, the *New York Daily News*, the *Cape Cod Standard-Times*, the Boston newspapers, the *Christian Science Monitor*, the *Wall Street Journal*, the *Worcester Gazette*. In addition, he had discovered a few odd, new ones: the *National Observer* and the *Herald*. And, of course, on the days it appeared, the *Vineyard Gazette*. This was one of those days, and as was his habit, he put all the others aside to consider the *Gazette*. Over the mast-head there was a poetic line, as always, a feature of the paper as far back as he could remember. He had come to think of it as an American form of haiku. Today it read: "Blackberries! Thick on stickery canes, where wild vines grow rank, In tangled abandon, They dangle from branches. Ethel Jacobson." Not bad. His eyes scanned the headlines: "E.Y.C. 48TH ANNUAL REGATTA HAS MIXED YACHTING WEATHER." As usual. "G. C. WUERTH; CAME TO ISLAND IN 1913." Oh, dear. Another friend gone. "GAY HEADERS ANNOYED BY MYSTERY PLANES' BUZZING." What? He looked at the front-page photograph. An Airedale.

Then, suddenly, he was struck by another headline. It came up from the page with such force and velocity that he literally flinched.

A sound, somewhere between a moan and a gasp, escaped him.

He closed his eyes, hard, for a time, reopened them and read again:

Japanese House to Rise
on Squibnocket Pond

Authentic Wood Replica
Already Under Construction

A story followed, but he did not read it. He got out of bed and showered, but could not shave because his hands were trembling. He dressed hastily, settling finally on a turtle-neck shirt when he found he could not knot his necktie. He drank a cup of coffee, sat down, and made a firm effort to collect himself. His behavior of late had been exemplary. There had been no more than a single lapse when he had reversed the to and from addresses on a letter to Jacqueline and was surprised, the following day, to receive a letter from himself. As to the pond project, he had long since put it out of his mind, and had not, for years, thought of it seriously. What could this announcement mean, if indeed it was an announcement and not his sick imagination at work? At play? He had learned by now that deterioration is neither neat nor ordered. Mind and body do not wear out in tandem. He knew that either his physical being or his mental capacity would give out first. He had hoped it would be his body. He decided to look at the paper once again, to make certain. He picked it up. There was no mistaking it:

Japanese House to Rise
on Squibnocket Pond

His next thought was that it was all an elaborate joke of some kind. Who would perpetrate it? He could not think. His brain was congealed. It *was* a joke. A single copy with this inserted. They do things like that these days. Of course. He smiled. Pretty funny, at that.

He walked to Falmouth, to the newspaper store. The stack of *Gazettes*. He looked at them. All the same. There it was.

He went to the dock and boarded the little *Island Queen*. An hour later, he got into a taxi and was driven to Squibnocket Pond. He instructed the driver to wait, and walked into his wood. Nothing. The hatchdoor that had, an eternity ago, held picnic supplies, had been pushed aside and the locker ransacked. Kids? Who cares? But the story in the *Gazette* was a fabrication. He knew it.

He became aware of the vibrant music of carpentry.

234

Rhythmic hammers and a counterpoint of singing saws. His imagination again?

"Oh, Christ!" he said aloud and grasped his head, covering his ears. He sat on a stump for a long time. When he released his head, the sounds were still in the air and he knew, beyond doubt, that they were real.

He made his way, pulled magnetically, toward the sound. It proved to be a long journey to the opposite side of the pond. He tore his clothes on brambles and thorns, fell into marsh, slipped on a cluster of mossy rocks, hit his forehead, and bloodied his face, but went on.

He reached a hedgerow. Beyond it, screened by underbrush, activity could be discerned. On his hands and knees, he crawled through, stood up, and saw it. A Japanese house, under construction. He fell to his knees and regarded it. It was larger than the one he had once planned, but lovely in proportion and line. The gardens around it, still in layout stage, were beautiful.

So intent was he in his study of the structure, that it was some time before he shifted his attention to the workers. There were six. Three men, two of them bearded, all of them long-haired, wearing the briefest of denim shorts. The other three were girls, also in shorts, also stripped to the waist. Were they? Yes. All six people in efficient action.

He stood up and moved toward them.

One of the girls saw him first and screamed. The sounds stopped. The workers froze.

"What the hell?"

"All right, all right. Cool it. I'll handle it."

"Be careful."

"Are you kidding? It's nothing. Some old bum. Lost, probably."

"Don't go alone, Rip."

"Will *you* buzz off?"

"Lookin' for somebody, Pop?"

"I'm Freeman Osborn."

"Yuh?"

"I'm the owner of the property across the pond."

"Yuh?"

From afar: "What does he want?"

"Nothing. Get back to work." To Freeman: "So?"

"How does it happen," asked Freeman, "that you're building a Japanese house?"

"We're all Japanese, that's why."

A girl approached. "Tell him to go away, Rip. We're not *dressed*, for Christ's sake."

"Tell him yourself."

"Go '*way*, mister. We're not *dressed*."

Freeman took off his hat.

"What is so strange," he said calmly, "is the fact that *I* was going to build a Japanese house on this pond. In fact, I have material for it—imported—in storage at Carroll's right now. I went there—to Japan—and bought it myself."

"Is that so?" the young man commented.

"Why didn't you?" asked the girl.

"Well—too long to tell. Complications and—but it was the dream of my life."

"O.K., Pop. Thanks for dropping in. Now drop out," said the young man.

"I went to Japan, you know, and brought back—did you ever hear of Gaisha Muto?"

236

"No."

"A fine architect. Great, maybe. He's dead now."

"Okay. See you." And to the girl: "Let's go, assy."

Freeman said, "I'd love to show you my plans and specifications."

"I can hardly wait to miss 'em," said the young man.

"Good," said Freeman. "I'll bring them over."

"The guy's a riot," said the girl.

"I wonder," said Freeman, "if someone could give me a lift to my taxi?"

"Oh, Jesus," said the girl.

"Sure," said the young man. "Come on."

Freeman got into a jeep with the young man. As they drove, Freeman talked about the Horyuji Temple at Nara, but the young man did not seem to be interested, so he stopped.

The taxi driver was shocked when he saw the condition of Freeman's clothing, face, and hands.

"What happened?" he asked. "An accident?"

"No," said the young man. "But keep an eye on him, will you? You keep letting him loose and he'll get himself hurt."

"Thanks," said Freeman.

"Goodbye, Pop."

The driver started back to Oak Bluffs, but Freeman insisted on Edgartown. He had business there, went directly to the Edgartown National Bank. When his friend Olive Hillman saw him, she took him at once to Dr. Nevin's office. The cut on Freeman's forehead required three stitches.

The taxi was dismissed.

Miss Hillman telephoned Falmouth and explained the situation.

Freeman spent the night at the doctor's house.

In the morning, provided with fresh clothes from Brickman's and a razor from the Colonial Drug Store, he was ready to proceed with his mission.

He went to his vault at the bank and selected a number of large envelopes containing material pertinent to his Japanese house project. He proceeded to Coby's office and from his files there extricated further plans and photographs and specifications.

In an Edgartown taxi, he made the trip back to the pond. Was he in the right place? A fence had been erected overnight, with a locked gate. A sign read:

LAFCADIO HEARN COMMUNE

KEEP OUT!

O-U-T

THIS MEANS YOU!

Y-O-U

RING BELL IF YOU

HAVE A REASON BUT

YOU DAMN WELL BETTER

HAVE A REASON

Lafcadio Hearn Commune Security Committee

238

Freeman pressed the bell button. In the distance, he heard it ring loudly.

A few minutes later, the jeep approached. Freeman waved his roll of plans at it. It stopped. The driver alighted, not the one he had met yesterday. This one was beardless and seemed angry as he asked, "What do *you* want?"

"I was here yesterday," said Freeman. "I talked to your friends . . ."

"What about it?"

"I have these plans I want to show you people. The Japanese house we were—I was planning to build on Squibnocket Pond. We."

"Look, fella. Can I give you some advice?"

"Of course."

"Don't be a pain in the ass. We're busy here. We're working. Don't be buggin' us!"

"I meant it in the friendliest—"

"Sure, sure—but who's got the time? Y'know? Maybe later."

"All right," said Freeman.

"Or maybe never."

"It's really a remarkable house. Ours was. Is."

"Two cheers," said the young man.

He moved away, got into the jeep, and backed it into the woods at breakneck speed.

XXXIII

SOME WEEKS (MONTHS? DAYS?) LATER, in Falmouth, Freeman, tired out, sat in his accustomed rocker, and found himself considering, reconsidering, that adventure. They were right, he *had* been a nuisance, they were at work. They would finish it someday. He would still be a land neighbor. He wondered if they would ever invite him in. If they did, would he go? He might. He would love to see the interior. And then again, he might not. Depended. On what? Who knows? Sheila. He watched the slow sunset.

He would tell her about it tonight. He was now talking to her nightly. Some people might think that crazy, but he wasn't crazy. He knew Sheila was dead—to everyone, but not to him. He had a way of talking to her. He would tell her. He smiled.

The screen door behind him slammed, jarring him. (Why do they always let it *slam* so?)

"Beautiful night, isn't it?" someone said. (Man? Woman?)

"Yes, it is."

Freeman returned to his thoughts. Why had they been so rude, those young people at the pond? He had only been trying to be friendly, trying to help. They might have learned something. He might have given them all the stuff out of storage if they had been civil. The countless hours that had gone into *his* house—

time and travel and money. Those damned young mugwumps—and didn't one of them call him an old bum? And that one with her bare chest hanging out. What the hell did *she* have to be so sassy about? Her endowments weren't all *that* good. He'd seen better. What was that they used to say? About tits? Something funny. What's the difference? The difference is the terrifying chasm that lies between remembering and not remembering. Try to recall it. Try. Press. Harder. No. No use. Wait. "Boopers." Yes! "There are sub-nubbins, nubbins, boopers, droopers, and super-droopers." He laughed, not so much at the line, but delighted that he had been able to remember it. What did *she* have to be so fresh about? She and her sub-nubbins. And their house wouldn't be a patch on the one he—. Sheila. Sheila's breasts appeared before his eyes. Perfection. So beautifully proportioned, full and bursting with life, so arousing. His fingertips remembered them; his tongue tasted them. He was getting dizzy. God damn! What if he went ahead and built their house after all? Wait. Hadn't everything been turned over to Jacqueline? Yes, but she'd see him through. He was sure of it. He would tell her what the doctor—one of the doctors—had told him the other day (last year?): "There's nothing more important for you, Mr. Osborn, than activity. Physical, mental, emotional. Do you see? Exercise. Walking. Do you ride a bike? Try it. More important still is the memory muscle—not a muscle, of course, but I like to call it that. I notice you read poetry. Do you ever memorize any? You should try. And learning. Anything. Some skill. Manual or otherwise. We should, all of us, never stop learning. It keeps the vital functions resilient—the way walking keeps the leg muscles and the circulatory system in shape. Mrs. Roosevelt, I read somewhere recently, started piano lessons at seventy-three. Stay involved, Mr. Osborn. Don't ever allow yourself to vegetate. In geriatrics these days, we say: 'Add life to years, not just years to life!' Isn't there some project that would interest you? Why not undertake it? Action!"

Freeman felt his skin tingling. What was it Ed Tyra had last told him about the total cost? $110,000. Impossible. His own estimate had been just under 30. Yes, but that was in the beginning. That was a long time ago. That was—when? What is it now? 1950 something. No. '60. It is 1973. 1974? And when did Ed say 110? And when was it 30? His head was beginning to ache. He got up out of the chair and started in to the lobby.

"Calling it a night, Doc?" (Woman? Man?)

"Not quite."

He closed the screen door quietly (it could be done, he noted) and went up the stairs, one at a time. In his bedroom, he went to his knees and, with some difficulty, pulled the footlocker out from under his bed. He had emptied the vault at the Edgartown bank—too far, too hard to get to—and now had his things here. His things. All that was left of his life, he reflected, contained in one tin box and his head. The footlocker held, in neatly banded and marked legal folders, the remaining documents of record. "J.O." "FINAN," "WALPOLE PEN.," "STORE," and so on. He found the folder marked "SQUIB PND," removed it, and returned the footlocker to its place.

He took the Squibnocket material to his writing

table, adjusted the Tensor lamp (a birthday gift from his eldest grandson), put on his reading glasses, found his magnifier, and began to pore over the documents. His determination increased, his confidence swelled, and he felt stronger than he had in a year. Aloud, he spoke a Ben Franklin maxim to which Henry Hough had once called his attention: "Resolve to perform what you ought; perform without fail what you resolve."

He became deeply immersed in the sketches and revisions and notes and specifications and correspondence and estimates and plans. Plans. Plans. Hours (days?) passed. His eyes tired. He should put these back into the footlocker. He *had* put them back and taken them out again—more than once. Time had passed. How much? Put them back, they can always come out again. No. He had not done with them. Leave them where they are. No need for all this endless in and out. Safe here? Of course. Who on earth would be interested in any of this junk? Junk? No. He looked at the alarm clock beside his bed. Late. Whatever day it was, whatever season, it was long past his bedtime—but he was far from ready for bed. He would go down and watch the sunset. No. It had already set. Oh, well. There would be another, there always was. He would go down anyway. Perhaps the sunrise. That was more in line with his present mood, in any case. Yes. The sunrise. Sheila was especially fond of sunrises. They had shared many. Not enough, but some. The one in London after the V-E Day all-night celebrations. The world of reason being reborn before their eyes. Had she been with him that night? Yes. No? And that one in Japan— had they been together? He could not be certain, dredged his memory, decided affirmatively. But the best was the one that had awakened them the first night they spent at the pond. That one, too, suggested rebirth, but of them as a pair. *Any* sunrise was worth waiting for, worth living for. He went downstairs, moving hurriedly, not pausing, this time, on each one of the stairs.

"Still up, Mr. Osborn?" (A different person? Yes. Man.)

"Still up."

He returned to his rocker. He squinted at the sky, which was powdered with stars. He estimated a couple of hours to sunrise. He had a way of knowing that involved sight and sound, the state of the dew, the touch of the atmosphere on his skin.

Spring had turned to winter. (More than once?)

He was alone on the porch. It was still. A faraway owl, hooting mournfully, shared his predawn vigil. Was the owl, too, remembering?

Freeman picked up the broken thread of his thought. He had learned to do this in recent years.

Plans, he brooded. Plans. His whole long (too long?) life had been largely plans. Did any of them pan out? Plan out? No, *pan* out. Did any of them happen? Come to—what's the word? Damn! Come to—like food—an "f"—harvest—fruit—*fruition!* Did any of them come to fruition? Not many. Some. Small ones. Mosquitoes. The discovery. What was it called? Something something. Two words. Which two? Hell with it. None of the big plans made it. Well, the planning was life, too. He and Sheila on the floor with the blueprints and the excitement and then—did it happen?—on the floor?

244

On the blueprints? Those very ones in the vault—no, *upstairs!* Yes. And now our plan has materialized, come to—fruition. A Japanese house on Squibnocket Pond. Yes, but not ours. Not mine and Sheila's. Does it matter? Probably not. *Certainly* not! The fact is, there it is.

He had seen it, done, finished, beautiful. Had he?

He looked up at the moon. It was full. Does it matter, in the end, who first sets foot on the moon? Name or nation?

(Hadn't there been something on TV and in the papers about someone doing just that, not long ago?)

The point is—*someone* gets to the moon. *Someone* builds a Japanese house on Squibnocket Pond. That is the point.

Sheila.

He smiled, then he laughed softly. A moment later he began to cry.

"Are you all right?"

It was the voice of Mrs. Weidenfeld, the night attendant. He waved her away.

"Shouldn't you be in bed?" she persisted. "What are you doing out here, anyway?"

He turned to her and bellowed, "I'm laughing and crying! Now go away! Go to bed yourself!"

He kept his eyes on her as she went through the screen door—it slammed like a gunshot—and saw her approach Petey, fat and mulled, playing solitaire at the desk.

Freeman listened.

"*He's* not long for this world," said Mrs. Weidenfeld.

"Who?"

"Old Osborn."

"Oh, *he's* okay," said Petey. "Leave 'im alone."

Freeman turned back to the sky. The sun was coming up. He stopped laughing, and a few minutes (months? years?) later, he stopped crying.